Haunted Horse Camp

Hey Friend!

Yay, you're here! We're so happy you're coming along on our spooky horse adventure! This is only our second mystery, so we need your help! I mean, we're comedians, NOT detectives! Join us as we ride horses, get lost in the spooky woods, and... see a ghost horse!

Now, let's stop horsin' around and have some fun!

Love,
The Sister Detectives

GISELLE   **E**VANGELINE   **M**ERCEDES

GEM Sisters™

Hang Out With GEM Sisters

Join the club!
www.gemsisters.club

Watch on YouTube
 /gemsisters

GEM
MAIL

Write to us!

GEM Sisters
P.O. Box 3062
Glendale, CA 91221

Horse Play!

"Evangeline run!" screamed Mercedes.

As fast as they could, the girls sprinted across Graveyard Hill.

Giselle ran in front of the stable doors. "This way! Over here!" she yelled, motioning to her sisters.

That's when she saw it. Through the smoky mist, a white glowing horse burst out from the middle of the herd. It was headed straight for them.

Giselle screamed to her sisters, "Faster! It's right behind you!"

Mercedes didn't look back. She and Evangeline could barely breathe. They ran faster than ever before. Left! Right! Left! Right! Left! Right!

Giselle rushed over to the stable door and started to close it. Mercedes and Evangeline were almost there, but so was the Ghost Horse.

In a flash, her sisters fell inside. Giselle shut the door with all her might. *SLAM!*

Safely inside, the girls fell to the ground. Their hearts wouldn't stop pounding.

"I can't believe it," gasped Giselle. "The Ghost Horse . . . is real!"

Sister Detectives

Haunted Horse Camp

By MéLisa Lomelino
& Ryun Hovind

MéLisa and Ryun Productions
Los Angeles, CA

For Valerie.
Thank you for believing in us
and for dreaming as big as we do.

ISBN-13: 978-1-947775-02-2
ISBN-10: 1947775022
ISBN-13 eBook: 978-1-947775-03-9

First Printing: September 2018
Manufactured in the United States of America.
MéLisa and Ryun Productions
P.O. Box 3062
Glendale, CA 91221

To see GEM Sisters' videos visit: youtube.com/gemsisters
To see behind the scenes of GEM Sisters check out their website: GEMSisters.club

Contents

CHAPTER 1

VRRROOMMM!

A crowded minivan full of film gear sputtered down a small country road. The traffic jams and city lights of Los Angeles were now replaced with empty streets and overgrown trees. The sun would be setting soon, and the entire GEM Sisters' family wished they were already at Spirit Horse Camp.

GEM Sisters were three real life sisters with beautiful brown skin. They were famous for their funny videos. The word GEM stood for their initials: Giselle, Evangeline, and Mercedes.

In the back seat Giselle, 14, was sleeping with her mouth wide open. As she tossed and turned, her short hair stuck to her face. She snored loudly as her sisters giggled.

Mercedes' hazel eyes sparkled like the

sequins on her pink dress. She was 10 years old and full of sass. She didn't flinch as she held out her phone and snapped a picture of Giselle sleeping.

She giggled, "Hey Evangeline. How about the caption, *I eat drool for dinner.*"

Evangeline, 9, was the youngest of the three sisters. She had an imagination as wild as her clothes. She grinned as she looked at the picture. For a split second she felt bad, then she came up with a joke.

"Caption the picture, *Dreaming of Prince Charming*," replied Evangeline, laughing at the small puddle of drool on Giselle's arm. "The fans would love that!"

"And post," said Mercedes.

This week the family was heading to Spirit Horse Camp in the deep woods. Mom and Dad owned a video production company and hoped to one day make big Hollywood movies. For now, they filmed whatever projects they could get to pay the bills.

"Here comes a bump in the road," said Dad as he drove.

The van bounced and jolted Giselle awake.

Mercedes quickly put down her phone and changed the subject, "So who is this guy you are filming at the camp?"

Mom replied, "His name is Callahan Wilcox. He's famous for hosting his show *Animal Hauntings.*"

"Famous? How many followers does he have?" asked Evangeline.

Mom continued, "Callahan is 'Cable TV famous' not 'Internet famous'. Honestly he's a little weird and creepy."

"But he's paying us, so let's be nice. And let's keep our spirits up," Dad laughed at his own joke. "Get it? Spirits? Spirits, ya know, like ghosts?"

Dad was always making jokes hoping for a laugh. He usually wouldn't give up until he got one.

Then he said in a low, scary voice, "But seriously, bewaaaaarrre. We're gooooing to a haaaauuuunted horse caaaaaamp. Aaaaaaahhh!"

Mercedes looked up with a scowl. "Dad can we just not? I don't even like thinking about ghosts."

Giselle saw an opportunity to tease her sister. "What do you find scarier? Ghosts or spiders?"

"I don't know," Mercedes said with a smirk,

"but I think it's scary how many likes you have on this picture I just posted."

"Mom!" whined Giselle. "Mercedes posted a picture of me sleeping. With my mouth open!"

Mercedes stuck out her tongue at Giselle. "Now we're even for the picture you posted of me when I had lettuce in my teeth."

"Be nice you two," Mom said as she read a book, not really listening.

Mom and Dad were used to Giselle and Mercedes being at war on social media. It was a battle that never ended, so they didn't take sides.

Evangeline jumped in, "I think ghosts are awesome. I can't wait to make friends with them! How are you guys gonna film 'em anyway?"

"I brought my night vision goggles, low light cameras, and motion sensors," said Dad. "If anyone can catch ghosts on video, it's this dude."

Mercedes looked more nervous than ever. Her voice squeaked, "Catch them? Now you're catching the ghosts?"

Mom replied, "Okay everyone, settle down." She gave Dad a *knock-it-off* look.

"We're not catching ghosts, sweetie. We're

just filming them. Or, I mean, filming whatever scary stuff happens," continued Mom.

Mercedes' voice went high. "Wha— wha— what kind of scary stuff?"

Dad smiled at Mom with a *you-really-goofed-that-up* look. He added, "Mercedes, ghost shows are usually more mystery than scary. It's just a normal horse camp with a fun legend. I doubt we'll see anything."

Mercedes instantly felt better. "Good because I am only going to this camp for one reason. So I can learn to—"

"Ride horses!" said everyone in the van at the same time. "We know!"

Mercedes hadn't stopped talking about the announcement for weeks. A new TV show called Horse Divas was accepting auditions.

"Um how are you submitting an audition? You don't know how to ride a horse," asked Giselle smugly.

"I'm Mercedes. I'll figure it out!" she replied with a snap of her fingers.

Suddenly a horrible smell filled the minivan.

"Every time we travel girls. Seriously! Every time!" said Mom as she rolled down her window.

"I just woke up. It wasn't me!" said Giselle.

"That's not true. You could have been sleep farting," said Evangeline with a raised eyebrow.

"Okay, settle down ladies," said Dad. "No mystery to solve here. I just got hungry and opened a hardboiled egg."

For a second they thought Dad knew their secret. The girls' parents still didn't know that they solved mysteries together as the Sister Detectives. They decided to keep it a secret because they didn't want their parents to worry.

Mom groaned at Dad. "Well don't keep eating the egg. Throw it out the window! It smells!"

Dad quickly shoved it in his mouth, "Scheee? There'shh no more schmelll!"

Mom gagged and looked away as small bits of egg flew out of Dad's mouth.

The whole family was excited to spend an entire week at camp. The GEM Sisters had decided in advance not to film any funny videos or solve any mysteries. The only plan they had was to make lots of memories.

"How many more minutes?" asked Evangeline, who was the most excited to get there.

"According to my phone it says 'quit asking',"

Mom replied. "When we get there you'll know it!"

Evangeline sighed in defeat. That answer might as well have been ten jillion hours. She pulled out two books from her rainbow colored backpack.

"Should I read, 'The Ghost Who Needed A Hug', or 'How To Potty Train A Ghost?'" asked Evangeline.

Giselle shook her head, "I guess the hug one?"

Mercedes nodded in agreement.

"Great! Potty training it is," Evangeline replied doing the opposite. She hugged her new ghost stuffed animal and turned to the first page.

Giselle scrolled on her tablet. "I read something online about the camp you might find interesting."

"Doubt it," said Mercedes, half listening while making cute faces on her phone. She was not interested in another one of Giselle's boring school stories.

"This website is all about the history of the Native Americans who used to live at Spirit Horse Camp. Well they didn't live at the camp, they lived on the land where the camp is now.

You see, the legend starts with a warrior boy—"

"We're here!" interrupted Dad.

The entire van cheered.

A large sign hung over a small dirt road. It read "Spirit Horse Camp." The van kicked up a lot of dust as it drove into camp. The girls looked out the cloudy van windows and saw that the forest grew all the way up to one side of the road. On the other side was a large fenced-in pasture filled with horses.

There were silky brown colts and black as night stallions. The girls oohed and aahed over the different colors and sizes. Then Giselle laid eyes on the most beautiful creature she'd ever seen.

"Who is that hunk?" muttered Giselle, a little too loudly.

Riding one of the horses was a lean, muscular boy with long black hair pulled into a ponytail. He looked like he'd come straight from a movie.

"Gross," said Evangeline. Boys were definitely not on her radar, unless she was beating them in video games.

As the van drove on, the boy and the horses got smaller and smaller. Giselle strained to see him. He was twirling a lasso and riding the horse like a pro. She was surprised to see a boy since this was an all girls' camp. Good thing she had packed her cutest outfits.

"Yee-haw!" Dad yelled as he skidded to a stop in front of the log cabin office.

Dad opened the door to get out, and a cloud from the dusty road flew in. Mom and the girls coughed. Dad poked his head back in, acting as if he didn't know them.

"Well, howdy cowgirls!" he said to the back seat. Then, turning to their mom, he asked, "And aren't you just about the cutest thing this ole' cow poke has ever seen?"

Mom looked back at him, batting her eyelashes. "Why hello there handsome stranger. I've never met a real cowboy before."

Dad leaned over to kiss Mom and the girls all looked away.

The smell of horse poop now filled the air. The sisters tried to breathe through their shirts. They couldn't decide what was worse. The smell, or their parents kissing.

"Greetings night owls. Finally, you're here!" said a loud but serious voice. "I can't wait to start filming the newest episode of *Animal Hauntings*."

It was Callahan Wilcox, the *famous-to-some-*

people TV host who had a flair for drama. He was a short man with pale skin and slicked back gray hair. Mercedes wondered what kind of product he used to get that greasy look.

The family got out of the car and were greeted by a tall, wise looking, Native American man. He was older and had long gray hair. He wore tan clothes covered in bright beads.

Another woman reached out her hand to greet them. She had long black hair and brown skin with deep brown eyes. She was wearing tan shorts and a buttoned-up white shirt that read "Spirit Horse Camp". She was definitely the one in charge.

"Welcome GEM Sisters," said the woman. "My name is Miss Amy and I run this camp."

Mom and Dad shook hands with Miss Amy and introduced themselves.

Miss Amy continued, "This is the camp's owner and my grandfather, Chief Black Feather."

The chief thought carefully before he spoke. As he opened his mouth, Callahan interrupted.

"Guys, can you feel it? There's something in the air. The ghosts are ready for their close-ups. Come with me, cameraman," said Callahan, motioning to Dad.

"Hold up," stated Miss Amy. "You have to check in first. If we had a computer system, I would just slap bracelets on you, scan them, and be done in five minutes.

The chief interrupted her, "The old ways have always worked. Besides, a computer cannot live in the woods."

Dad opened the back of the van and started unloading. He handed each GEM Sister a suitcase, 1, 2, 3, 4 . . . 5? Why were there five?

"Mercedes!" Dad said annoyed. "We all agreed, one suitcase."

"I did. One suitcase for shoes, one for my clothes, and one for accessories."

Evangeline gave her Dad a loving pat on the shoulder. "Trust me. As Mercedes' roommate, I've learned it's best to get things in writing."

Amy frowned and picked up Mercedes' extra two suitcases. They started walking to the cabin.

Callahan put his arm around Dad and whispered in his ear, "Do you know what scat is?"

Dad replied, "Uh yeah, it's animal poop."

Callahan smiled as if he was hiding a secret. "Exactly. Well I found ghost scat. Grab a camera and c'mon."

"Have fun girls," Mom yelled to them just before she went inside the office with the chief. "I brought you extra clean underwear, just in case. Let me know if you need them."

"Gotta go mom, bye!" said Giselle walking faster to her cabin. A handful of campers were definitely hearing this and she did not want her mom embarrassing them anymore.

They arrived at an old broken down cabin. The roof was sagging, the cabin logs were weather-worn and cracked, and one of the windows was broken.

"Hashtag Creepy," said Giselle, who had expected a nicer cabin.

"Hashtag Spiders," Mercedes said in horror as she looked at the front door.

"Hashtag Awesome," said Evangeline, as she poked her finger in a large gooey web on the porch.

"I can't possibly sleep here," said Mercedes dramatically. "I'll get bit by a poisonous spider! I'll die before I get a chance to ride horses!"

"Actually," Giselle said, hoping this scientific fact would impress her sisters. "Although most spiders have venom, it's too weak to hurt humans. They just use it to paralyze their insect prey."

"Giselle you can stay out here and write an essay," said Evangeline pushing the front door open. "I'm going in!"

"Wait!" called out Mercedes. "I'm going first. Then the icky spiders will drop on you."

The girls argued until Miss Amy whistled loudly.

"Ladies how about we all just go in together?" She opened the door, motioning them inside.

The GEM Sisters walked in and instantly saw what looked like the best slumber party ever. The cabin was filled with girls their ages, colorful sleeping bags, and cute pillows with cartoon pillowcases.

The cabin was crowded with parents and soon-to-be friends. This was going to be so much fun! One of the moms was braiding her daughter's blonde hair. Another mom was making her daughter's bed. A dad was nervously reminding his daughter to be careful of a long list of camp hazards. Another poor dad, not wanting to leave, stood by the door with a single tear in his eye.

"Attention campers," said Amy loudly for all to hear. "We have some new friends I want to introduce."

"OMG! GEM Sisters!" a girl shouted before Miss Amy could continue.

All the girls in the cabin came running over to say hi and exchange hugs.

"I can't believe it! I watch all of ya'lls videos," said a cute girl in cowboy boots with a strong southern accent. Her red pigtails shook as she held out her hand. "The name's Trudy. Glad to meet y'all!"

Evangeline gave Trudy a high five. Giselle reached out and gave her a hug.

"Hi GEM Sisters!" squealed the girl with blonde braids and big blue eyes. "I'm Emma and I run your fan account GEMS4Life. I literally can't breathe. I'm so excited to meet you!"

"Hi Emma, I really like your hair!" said Mercedes with her million dollar smile.

Emma almost fainted. "I can't believe we're roommates! What bunk are you going to pick, Mercedes? The one under mine is empty," she said hopefully.

Mercedes tried to hide feeling let down, but didn't do it very well. "I really wanted a top bunk."

"Yeah, I was here last year. I learned that you gotta come early for a top bunk," explained

14

Emma.

Mercedes wanted a top bunk because she was scared of spiders, but was too embarrassed to tell people. So she decided to lie.

She leaned in close, as if to tell Emma a big secret. "I don't want to sleep on the bottom bunk. Because one time I did, and I sat up too fast, and cut my head. I had to get . . . stitches!" She gasped. "And now I have . . . a scar!" she said in a horrified voice.

"Completely hidden by your hair," Giselle said annoyed.

Mercedes continued, "It's under my hair, true. But still. It's just awful, all bumpy and gross! What if it was on my face?"

"You can have my top bunk," offered Emma. "And I could take the one under yours if that's okay," Emma paused for a moment. "Unless Giselle or Evangeline wants it, of course."

"Nope, they're fine," Mercedes answered for them.

Evangeline and Giselle watched as Emma began dragging Mercedes' heavy suitcases to their bed. Mercedes was so happy to make a friend, especially one that could lift heavy things. Mercedes sat on the top bunk and braided her hair to match her new bestie's.

Evangeline and Giselle locked eyes and shook their heads. Mercedes always seemed to get what she wanted. They settled in as bottom bunk buddies, finding two beds next to each other and putting their suitcases underneath.

The last parents in the cabin said their goodbyes. The final dad embarrassed his daughter by taking nonstop pictures before Miss Amy finally shoved him out the door. The girls all finished unpacking while they chatted and giggled.

Miss Amy whistled to get the girls' attention. "Tonight, on Graveyard Hill, we will have our opening ceremony. It's one of my favorite things at camp because we'll be making s'mores!"

The girls let out a squeal and hugged each other. Miss Amy started to tell the girls to grab their sweatshirts and bug spray when . . . the whole cabin went DARK!

"Aaargh!" The girls all screamed frightened. "Ghosts!"

"Girls! Calm down," instructed Miss Amy. "The cabin's light bulb went out. Get your flashlights."

One by one small beams of light filled the cabin. The girls went right back to giggling as they held the flashlights under their chins and made funny faces.

Miss Amy whistled again to get their attention. "Sorry, but you'll have to get used to things breaking. We keep camp costs down for your parents by not replacing things when they get old. Trust me. I don't like it either."

Emma spoke up, "Yeah, last year the lights went out like every night. Definitely keep your flashlight with you."

"Okay Emma," called out Miss Amy. "Since you were here last year, I want you to go to the main office and ask the chief for more light bulbs."

Emma replied, "Can I bring my new friend Mercedes?"

Mercedes quickly tried to think of an excuse. She did not want to walk around a dark camp with ghosts and spiders all around her.

Thankfully Miss Amy said no. "I can't have multiple kids wandering around after dark. It's a quick trip. Just hurry and when you get back, we can all leave for the opening ceremony."

Everyone could tell that Emma wasn't thrilled about going alone. She left slowly, clutching her flashlight as she walked out the door.

Miss Amy's phone rang.

"Hello," she said as her mouth turned to an angry frown. "If the toilet overflows when you flush it, then don't flush it! The water's going everywhere? Seriously? Ugh. I'll be right there."

She hung up and the girls all let out a nervous giggle.

"I'm sorry. I have to go take care of this. I will be right back and then we will go to the ceremony," Miss Amy said as she ran out the door.

Evangeline opened her suitcase which was mostly filled with candy. She grabbed her ghost book and started reading by flashlight.

"Why did you bring so much candy?" asked Giselle.

"I'm not asking you about what you packed. Mind your own business," answered Evangeline.

The campers gathered in a circle and talked while they waited for Emma to return. They asked the GEM Sisters all types of questions. Mercedes explained that their parents were there to film a TV show about the Ghost Horse.

Trudy spoke up in a serious voice, "I heard last year one of the campers went out alone after lights-out to look for the Ghost Horse. She never came back."

Slowly all of the girls pointed their flashlights at the front door of the cabin. Emma still wasn't back. She had been gone a long time now.

They sat quietly, listening to the soft chorus of crickets chirping. Suddenly the crickets stopped. The girls' eyes grew wide. Something was wrong. They all froze in fear.

A loud horse cry echoed across the night air. Followed by a long panicked SCREAM!

Mercedes cried out in fear, "Oh no! The Ghost Horse has Emma!"

CHAPTER 2

Mercedes' face was flushed when she finally made it to Graveyard Hill. Her lungs ached and her head hurt from running so fast. The moonlight revealed her new friend Emma all alone. She was still shaking as she sat on a log.

"Emma you're okay!" yelled Mercedes, giving her a big hug.

The other campers were huffing and puffing right behind Mercedes. Everyone was relieved to see that Emma was safe. They surrounded her and asked what happened.

"It was so horrible," said Emma in tears. "I saw the Ghost Horse!"

Evangeline couldn't believe it. "I knew it was real!"

Just then a voice boomed from the darkness, getting closer as he spoke, "There she is. Quick! Get the camera over here."

It was Callahan, the TV show host. He was wearing a dark red cape. The GEM Sisters figured it was a costume for his show, but even so, it was cheesy.

"Young lady, I know you're terrified. So please, if you could just say that to the camera," said Callahan. He wanted the moment filmed for his TV show.

Suddenly a low growl came from the bushes as they shook. What was that? A dark form stumbled out. Everyone gasped. Was it another ghost?

"Ouch! Sorry, I got a thorn bush stuck to my behind," said Dad as he almost dropped the camera.

The GEM Sisters tried to hide their embarrassment with nervous laughter. Dad did a little wave to them and pulled out a thorn.

Callahan hurriedly motioned for Dad to start filming. He looked into the camera, holding up his cape to look like a vampire bat.

"Greetings night owls. I am standing on spooky Graveyard Hill. What you're about to see will shock you to your very core. You may tremble, you may turn your eyes away in horror, but you will never forget what you are about to hear," he said dramatically.

Mercedes held Emma's hand and encouraged her. "Emma you got this. Just tell us what happened."

Emma slowly started talking, "Well . . . I was going to the camp office to get a light bulb."

"So what you're saying," Callahan interrupted, "is that you were wandering the campgrounds alone after dark. A thick fog was on the ground. Moonlight crept through the clouds."

The campers turned their eyes to Callahan as he told the story. They were spellbound.

Emma looked at Callahan, making sure it was her turn to talk. "The chief wasn't at the office. I knew where he kept the light bulbs from last year, so I just grabbed one and headed back."

Callahan spoke up again, "So there you were, cold, alone, lost in the forest. Then . . . the moon went dark. It got quiet and your world went black."

Emma shook her head no and said, "I was super scared, but I wouldn't say that—"

Callahan was on a roll and ignored her, "You felt blind walking in complete darkness. You shook your flashlight frantically, tapping it over and over, but it wouldn't come on."

Emma's face shifted as she nodded in agreement. "Yes, actually. That is what happened."

She added, "I kept hitting the flashlight, but it would only flicker. I was freaking out. Then this terrible sound came from the trees."

Callahan nodded and then motioned for Dad to zoom into her face.

Emma's face filled with worry. "The horrible sound was like, I don't know, an elephant charging at full speed!"

Callahan finished the story for her, "The clouds parted as the murky moonlight played in the sky. There was no safe place to hide. What was that coming out of the fog? No, it couldn't be!"

Everyone gasped. This guy could tell a good story. Even if he was wearing a cheesy cape.

Callahan held out his cape with one arm. "This, this . . . terrifying creature was a glowing, galloping horror with fire red eyes. It was the Ghost Horse. And it was coming straight for your soul!"

Emma jumped. "Yes! I literally felt an icy cold blast when the ghost flew by me."

The campers stood in shocked silence.

Emma started tearing up. She put her hands over her face. "I was almost trampled to death."

Out of nowhere Miss Amy appeared running and out of breath. She stepped in front of the camera. "Excuse me! You can't interview her. This poor girl is terrified." She put her arm around Emma to comfort her.

Callahan apologized and then smiled. He had the footage he needed.

Evangeline glanced over and saw Mom and the chief walk up. He had been giving mom a tour of the camp and telling her all about its long history.

Mom looked at Dad holding the camera, the scared kids, the host, and Miss Amy who appeared very frustrated. "What's going on?" Mom asked.

Mercedes answered with her usual sass, "Apparently you brought us to a camp where they leave kids alone in the woods to die!"

Miss Amy was about to defend what happened.

"You missed it!" Callahan yelled as he ran over to Mom, "Well, actually we all missed it! Except for this young lady who got the thrill of a lifetime."

"We were setting up the cameras when we heard the scream," added Dad. "Two seconds later and we would've been here to film the whole thing."

"I can still feel his ghostly presence in the air," explained Callahan. "The Ghost Horse will be back. Maybe even tonight at the ceremony."

Amy could see by the looks on the campers' faces that no one liked the idea of possibly seeing the ghost in person. "Girls, I'm sorry, but after what happened, I'm going to cancel the Opening Ceremony."

The campers let out a collective groan. Everyone had been excited about eating yummy s'mores.

Then Amy turned to Emma, "I know you're scared, and I know you think you saw something, but—"

Emma yelled stubbornly, "It wasn't something, it was the Ghost Horse!"

Chief Black Feather walked up to Emma and gently held her hand.

"You should be honored, young one. The Spirit Horse revealed himself to you. I am the only other soul that has seen him on this land."

Emma felt a lot of things, but honored was not one of them.

"I want to go home," said Emma. "This place is too scary."

Giselle, Evangeline, and Mercedes all rushed in and gave her a hug.

Callahan motioned to Dad to start filming. He turned the camera toward the chief and moved closer.

"Ladies and gentlemen, there are forces of evil out tonight. We are so lucky to have the only other person to see the Ghost Horse and live to tell the tale. Please, Chief Black Feather, give us every terrifying detail."

The chief sounded serious as he spoke, "This land we are standing on is called Graveyard Hill because it was built on the graves of my ancestors. They honored the animal spirits, and therefore the spirits honored them. Yes, the Powerful Warrior Spirit Horse has visited me. He only visits those who are pure of heart."

Everyone was quiet as the chief went on to tell his story.

"I was walking on Graveyard Hill calling out to the night sky. A cold smoky wind blew across the plains. I thought perhaps it was my time to die. But when I looked to the sky for the Great Spirit to take me away, I heard a mysterious sound."

Callahan interrupted, "Hey this is great stuff, really. But can you say something a little shorter, like 'the Ghost Horse stared into my soul'?"

Miss Amy had enough of all this filming nonsense. She whistled then spoke loudly, "Campers it has been an exciting night. But I promise you there is nothing to be scared of. These woods have strange sounds and flashes of light all the time. Now, everyone please return to your cabins and get ready for bed."

Mom grabbed Evangeline for a quick hug, "Are you okay? Are you scared?"

"No way Mom! This is the coolest camp ever," Evangeline said hugging Mom tighter.

Mom felt something hard in Evangeline's pockets as they hugged. Evangeline could tell she was about to get busted for candy. She quickly let go.

"Bye Mom! Love you!"

"Don't forget to brush your teeth," called out Mom.

Evangeline joined the girls from her cabin as they slowly walked together. She reached into her pocket and grabbed a lollipop then popped it into her mouth.

Giselle noticed the lollipop stick. "Did mom

say you can have that?"

"I'm at camp, which means this week I'm basically an adult so I can make my own decisions," replied Evangeline. "I gotta have something for my bedtime snack."

Giselle knew Mom wouldn't approve, but Evangeline was right. They were at camp and that meant making their own choices. She held out her hand for a lollipop.

"Strawberry Splash or Lemon Zing?" asked Evangeline. "Actually, take both. They taste really good when you put them in your mouth together!"

Giselle tried the two lollipops at once. "Yum!" Evangeline really did know a lot of secrets about snacks.

The group of girls arrived safely back at the cabin. They were much quieter than before as they all put on their pajamas. A lot of the girls were upset about the ceremony being canceled. Some of the girls were scared, but most were just annoyed.

Miss Amy sent the girls to use the bathroom in small groups. Finally it was the GEM Sisters' turn. They had Emma come with them and decided to bring extra flashlights . . . just in case.

Campground bathrooms were known to be a little scary, but this one was scarier than normal. A light bulb flickered, the sinks were scratched, and the stalls had possibly never been painted. The front door creaked as they all walked in.

"Really? More spiders?" said Mercedes. "Disgust-o-rama!"

SLAM!

Emma jumped as the door closed. She took a deep breath. "Thanks for walking with me. I don't want to be alone."

"Of course!" said Giselle, as she gave Emma a big hug.

Mercedes stared at a spider in the corner over the bathroom stall. "Are ghost spiders a thing? Because I've counted like three of them in this bathroom so far."

"Sadly, no," replied Evangeline. "That would be so cool but they don't exist. There are ghost animals and ghost people, but none of my books mentioned ghost insects."

"Guys, I don't think Emma wants to talk anymore about ghosts and made up stuff," said Giselle, as she turned on the sink.

"What do you mean by 'made up stuff'?" asked Emma.

"Giselle isn't a believer," answered Evangeline. "She thinks ghosts are dumb."

"I don't think they're dumb. They're just not real," said Giselle as she pulled her hair back in a headband. "It's science."

Mercedes stared into the mirror and moaned, "Does anyone else think this bad lighting makes my skin look like a green zombie?"

Evangeline looked in the mirror with her. "Nah. That's how you always look."

Mercedes rolled her eyes. "Ha ha, not funny. I need to look flawless for my audition video."

"Watch out zombie girl, you're getting a zit!" Evangeline said pointing to Mercedes' chin.

Mercedes looked in the mirror and panicked. Evangeline giggled. There was no zit.

The girls took turns at the sink. Giselle applied a face mask and washed off the blue sticky goo on her hands. She also didn't want any zits in case she saw the cute boy riding the horse tomorrow.

Giselle's face mask slowly started to dry, making it hard for her to move her mouth to talk. "Aw man!" she whined. "I should have brushed my teeth first."

Evangeline popped a jellybean into her

mouth. She wasn't brushing her teeth until the last possible second. She offered one to Emma. "Can I ask you a question? Why are you so scared of the Ghost Horse?"

"Because I don't want to become a ghost!" cried Emma.

"Hold up," said Mercedes, who had stopped brushing her hair. "What do you mean by 'become a ghost'?"

"You don't know?" replied Emma. "I thought all campers knew about the legend of the Ghost Horse."

"Sure. I read about it," said Giselle. "I saw a website about Native American legends. The tribe that used to live on this land has a myth about a great warrior. He rode a perfectly pure white horse. The horse was the protector of their land."

Evangeline raised her hand. "Is this gonna be one of your long stories?"

Giselle ignored her and continued, "There was this big battle and the warrior died to save his horse. The legend says that the spirit horse is looking for a new warrior, pure of heart, to help him protect this land."

"Exactly!" exclaimed Emma. "So if the Ghost Horse chooses you, he will touch you and turn you into a ghost!"

Mercedes dropped her brush in shock. "What? That's terrifying!"

Emma picked up Mercedes' brush for her. "Now do you see why I'm so scared?"

"Not really," answered Evangeline. "It's awesome. Like, you get to be a ghost! You can walk through walls. You can eat whatever snacks you want. Wait a sec. Do ghosts eat?"

Giselle wasn't buying it. She didn't believe you could be turned into a ghost. But she said nothing because she didn't want to hurt Emma's feelings. Not talking was easy now that her face mask had turned into rock hard clay.

Emma's face turned serious. "When the Ghost Horse looked at me, I thought I was done for. I'm not going to be able to sleep tonight. I want to go home!"

Mercedes put her arm around Emma. "Don't leave! We just got to meet you."

"I can't believe the Ghost Horse ruined my chance to be at camp with the GEM Sisters," sobbed Emma.

The sisters looked at each other and felt bad for Emma. They all came together for a group hug.

Just then Trudy poked her head in the door.

"Hey girlies! Miss Amy says ten minutes until lights out!" She noticed everyone was hugging. "Everything okay in here?"

Emma wiped her tears away.

"Should I take you to Miss Amy?" asked Trudy.

Emma nodded her head yes. She gathered her towel and toothbrush and walked out the door.

Giselle struggled to talk with the hard mask on her face. "You heard Trudy. We have ten minutes."

Evangeline knew she couldn't wait any longer. It was time to brush her teeth. She turned on the sink.

"Why does the water smell like farts?" she asked.

Giselle bumped her out of the way and started rinsing the mask off her face. "It's not farts. This camp uses well water, which contains minerals that react to bacteria and make hydrogen sulfide."

"Got it. Boring science lesson. The water still stinks like farts," replied Evangeline, holding her nose.

"Uh hello!" interrupted Mercedes. "We can't let this happen. We have to help Emma."

Giselle and Evangeline couldn't believe it. Mercedes was talking about someone other than herself.

"We can't let our fans down. Not ever," continued Mercedes. "Especially because if Emma leaves then she'll never get to watch me learn to ride a horse."

"Phew! That sounds more like you. For a second there you had me worried," joked Evangeline.

"I'm being serious," Mercedes said with a stern face. "Emma needs us. She needs the Sister Detectives."

"We agreed we weren't going to solve any mysteries this week. Besides, there's no actual case to solve," argued Giselle. "People think they see ghosts. But, it always turns out to be something like a car headlight or a weird-colored flashlight."

Giselle went back to washing her face. Evangeline sneakily picked up Giselle's toothbrush and quickly brushed her teeth. She put it back before Giselle noticed.

Mercedes gave her a questioning look. Evangeline whispered," I forgot to pack mine. Don't tell her or next time I'm using yours!"

Giselle reached for a towel and dried off her

face. Mercedes made a *my-lips-are-sealed* hand motion.

"Okay Giselle. If you're so sure then let's make a bet," said Evangeline. "If I'm right and the Ghost Horse is real, I'm going to make a shirt and you have to wear it in every GEM Sisters' video for a month."

"What's on the shirt?" asked Mercedes.

"Hmmm," said Evangeline. "It will read, I believe in ghosts now. Thanks Evangeline, you're way smarter than me!"

"Fine!" replied Giselle. "And when we prove I'm right, you have to wear a shirt that says, 'Science is cool and so is my sister Giselle.'"

"Is it supposed to embarrass you or her?" asked Mercedes.

"I'll figure it out later," said Giselle, flustered. "I'll think of something really good."

"Deal!" Evangeline said with attitude. She spit on her hand and grabbed Giselle's hand before she could pull it away.

"Gross!" said Giselle and Mercedes at once, not realizing Evangeline had meant a spit shake.

"So we're going to help Emma?" asked Mercedes.

"Yup," said Giselle, putting her toothbrush

in her mouth. She made a confused face. "Why is this wet?" she asked.

Mercedes and Evangeline smiled and shrugged their shoulders. The girls rushed back to the cabin just in time for lights out.

Mercedes leaned over her bunk and saw that Emma was already asleep. She whispered to herself, "Please don't leave Emma. We'll make sure you're safe. The Sister Detectives are on the case!"

CHAPTER 3

The next morning Evangeline woke up with a hand in her face. Actually there were two hands, three faces, and sixteen toes. It looked as if her stuffed animals had attacked her during the night and were now holding her hostage.

Mercedes was sleeping like an angel wearing a pink, fluffy eye mask. Giselle . . . not so much. Her face was buried in her pillow, and she was snoring louder than a chainsaw.

Miss Amy stood, already dressed by her neatly made bed. She glanced at her watch. The second it flipped to 6:00 am, she whistled, "Rise and shine ladies! You have 20 minutes to get up, get dressed, and get to the cafeteria for breakfast."

Everyone groaned. Campers pulled their sleeping bags over their heads.

"Life is so unfair," whined Giselle.

"I object!" complained Mercedes. "I need at least two hours for my morning routine."

"Now it's 19 minutes ladies," Miss Amy continued. "But the good news is, after breakfast, we will meet at the stables and see . . . the HORSES!"

That perked everyone up. They let out a tired cheer. "Yayyy!"

Evangeline was instantly dressed and ready. "Here's a tip Mercedes. Next time, sleep with your clothes on under your pj's. Then, you don't have to get dressed!"

"I have to go scare some raccoons out of the dumpster," said Miss Amy, "If the chief believed in motion sensor alarms, then I wouldn't have to. Anyway, I'll see you at the stables."

Mercedes leaned over her bunk to see how Emma was doing. "Hey girl. I hope you're feeling okay?"

To her surprise, Emma looked well rested. "I'm still scared, but I'm better. Thanks for being such a good friend yesterday."

"12 minutes!" yelled Evangeline as she checked her watch. "You better hurry."

The campers barely made it to the cafeteria on time. They sat at their table trying not to gag at the gross, gooey breakfast. Everyone that is, except Trudy.

"Ya'll ain't gonna eat yer eggs?" asked Trudy.

"Is that what this yellowish blob is?" asked Giselle.

The girls pushed their plates to Trudy. Evangeline reached into her pockets and shared her candy with everyone. It was fruit flavored so to Evangeline that was the same as fruit.

***

After breakfast the girls lined up outside the stables. The campers mostly wore jeans and t-shirts, which made Evangeline stand out like a cartoon character in the wrong movie.

She wore a crazy rainbow mix of clothes. Orange shorts with a blue striped top, mismatched knee high socks, and a headband with little poof balls that waved above her head like a bug's antennae.

"You wore that headband in a challenge video," said Emma. "It was so funny!"

A gust of wind blew by as Evangeline was about to say thank you. Evangeline made an odd face. Emma looked at her confused.

Evangeline's face kept curling into a weirder and weirder expression. Finally she sneezed, "Kablooey!"

"Bless you," responded Emma.

Evangeline sneezed again, "A la ka zooey!"

Heads turned with puzzled faces. What was Evangeline doing?

"Snur-Fa-Loo!" Evangeline blurted out another huge sneeze. "No it's not that either!"

"Um, what the heck kind of sneeze was that?" asked Giselle.

"Oh it's something new I'm trying," Evangeline said as if it were obvious. "I'm inventing the perfect sneeze. Remember when I sneezed last month? It really got me thinking."

"Who thinks about sneezing? You just do it," stated Mercedes.

"Well everyone says 'ah choo' when they sneeze. But why? Is it some kind of law? I want to invent a sneeze that sounds cooler. The perfect sneeze!"

Emma couldn't help but giggle. "I love your imagination Evangeline."

Mercedes sparkled in her hot pink outfit covered in glitter. She found the perfect camera angle to show off her new white leather boots. She pressed record on her phone.

"When I ride a horse I always dress to impress," said Mercedes with a smile. "That's just one of the many reasons you should choose me to be on *Horse Divas*." She blew the camera a kiss.

"Quick give me your phone," ordered Giselle. She grabbed the phone out of Mercedes' hands and held it up to her face like a mirror.

"I'm filming my audition!" argued Mercedes.

Giselle didn't care. She had forgotten to bring her own phone and needed to check herself. Nothing in her teeth. Nothing sticking to her face. No boogers. Phew!

She had a history of getting nervous and doing embarrassing things around cute boys. Giselle didn't want to take any chances, in case she saw that boy on the horse again.

Giselle admired herself in her cute outfit when Mercedes grabbed her phone back.

Mercedes was about to start filming herself again when Miss Amy whistled.

"Ladies! Great job making it on time," said Miss Amy as she checked her watch. "Wish I could say the same for your horse trainer."

All of a sudden, a black and brown horse burst out of the stables. The horse was running wild. The teen boy riding the horse could barely hold onto the reins.

"Help!" he yelled.

The horse galloped fast, then stood up on its back legs. He almost fell off, shouting in fear. He grabbed onto the side of the horse. His body barely holding on.

The girls screamed in fright.

The horse bounced him wildly as he ran circles around the girls. He struggled to pull himself back up.

"Hey Ty!" yelled Amy at the top of her lungs. "KNOCK IT OFF!"

"Whoa!" said Ty to the horse.

The horse came to a stop and Ty easily swung himself back up on the saddle.

"Girls, calm down. He's fine," explained Amy. "This is Ty, your horse trainer. He's also my very annoying little brother."

"It was just a prank, Amy. Lighten up," said Ty with a smile. "You don't always have to be the fun killer."

"Well you could try to grow up and not act like a kid," responded Amy.

Ty jumped off the horse and stood next to his sister. "I'm only 16. So actually I'm still a kid." He made a goofy face sticking out his tongue.

Giselle could not stop staring at Ty. His dark skin. His muscles. His long black hair that he pulled back in a ponytail. He was gorgeous!

Ty turned to the group of girls. "Hey guys! Never fear, I am here. And I will be bringing pranks, laughs, and most importantly . . . fun!"

The campers responded with smiles and a cheer. Amy rolled her eyes.

Giselle nervously shouted, "I love having fun! What's more fun than riding horses?" She didn't know what to do next, so she started clapping awkwardly. "Go horses!"

Mercedes and Evangeline shook their heads. They could tell Giselle had a crush on Ty, which meant they had to help her not look silly. To support their sister they joined Giselle in her odd clapping.

Ty looked at Giselle and smiled. Her heart instantly melted.

"Can we ride the horses now?" asked Mercedes. "Some of us have an important audition to film."

"Follow me," said Ty as he led the campers into the stables. "Before you can learn to ride a horse, you need to know how to take care of them.

Ty had the campers sit in a circle on bales

of hay. He gave a lesson on horse care which everyone found boring but Giselle. She was trapped in a love spell hanging on Ty's every word.

Ty explained that horses love to graze in the field for grass, but they also like to eat hay. He told the girls that horses have schedules just like people.

"You should try to feed your horse at the same time every day," explained Ty.

Evangeline didn't agree. She liked to snack all day long. In fact, it was time for her after breakfast snack. She pulled out a gooey gumball covered in pocket lint. She blew on it, then popped it in her mouth.

"Who has ridden a horse before?" asked Ty.

A couple girls raised their hands, including Trudy.

"Do you know the rule about feeding and exercising your horse?" Ty questioned.

Trudy waved her hand excitedly, then answered, "Horses gotta eat three hours after they exercise!"

"Correct," said Ty, as he gave Trudy a high five. "Can you help me show the group how to groom a horse?"

Giselle's heart sank. In that moment, she

wished she knew more about horses.

Ty led the girls to a stable with a brown horse covered in white spots. "This is Dot. You will take turns getting to ride her."

"Me!" Mercedes yelled as her hand shot up in the air.

Ty continued, "After you learn how to groom her."

Mercedes lowered her hand in defeat. This was starting to feel like school, which was not why she was here.

Ty held up a tool that looked like a rake. "Who knows what this is?" he asked.

"It's a horse poop scooper!" said Trudy, proud of herself.

The campers all giggled at the word poop. But to Giselle every word Ty said was like a love song.

Ty reached out and handed the poop scooper to Mercedes. "You want to ride horses so here ya go!"

Mercedes did not reach back. She pointed to her white boots, "These boots were made for riding, not raking. Pass!"

"I'll do it!" shouted Giselle. She ran up and grabbed the scooper.

Just then, Dot the horse raised her tail and

started pooping. All the girls held their noses. The horse kept pooping, and pooping, and pooping. Finally she finished.

Giselle's eyes grew wide as she looked at the giant smelly pile of poop.

"She must like you," Ty said to Giselle with a wink.

Giselle awkwardly smiled back. She was determined to show Ty she was good with horses. She held her breath and started to shovel. Suddenly, she felt Ty's hands on top of hers.

"Try to hold the handle like this," he explained.

Giselle wanted to melt into his arms. She pictured the two of them riding together off into the sunset. Her arms wrapped tightly around him.

Ty's voice snapped her out of her daydream. "Then you toss the poop into the muck bucket."

"Ewww!" The campers all groaned.

"Who wants to go next?" asked Ty. He handed the scooper to Trudy, the only girl with her hand raised.

"Greetings again night owls," came a voice lurking behind the group. It was Callahan, but without his cheesy red cape.

"Mr. Wilcox. I'm a huge fan!" said Ty as he walked up and shook his hand. "I've seen every episode of *Animal Hauntings*!"

"Always great to meet a fan," replied Callahan. "Maybe you could help me. I need to use the horses tonight for filming, but I can't find Miss Amy."

"If it's about horses then I'm your guy!" Ty answered excitedly.

Giselle couldn't believe Ty was a fan of Callahan. She decided to overlook this flaw. Ty was still nearly perfect.

Seeing Callahan reminded the Sister Detectives that they had a case to solve. The girls pretended to take turns scooping poop while they listened.

Callahan explained to Ty that tonight he wanted to have the horses grazing on Graveyard Hill for filming. "Sometimes ghost animals appear to other living animals. And it would make the perfect shot for the ghost reveal."

"That would look so cool," agreed Ty. "I'll do anything I can to help the show."

"Callahan, why are you back?" said Miss Amy as she entered the stables. "We just met this morning."

"We are going to use the horses in his TV show tonight," answered Ty excitedly.

"Absolutely not!" said Miss Amy.

"You can't tell me what I can do on my own time," replied Ty.

"We'll talk about this later," groaned Amy. "Right now, you need to teach the campers."

"Until tonight fellow night owl," said Callahan as he left.

The campers tried not to stare while Amy glared at Ty.

"Okay girls," said Ty, ignoring Amy. "I'm going to split you up into two groups. Grooming horses and mounting horses."

Mercedes had no interest in brushing a horse's hair. Especially the tail, it was way too close to where the poop had just come out. Gross!

"At least I can learn how to get on a horse," said Mercedes to her sisters.

"Did you hear what Callahan said?" asked Evangeline. "He thinks the Ghost Horse will appear tonight."

"Yeah," Giselle answered. "And mom and dad are going to film it."

"One of my books actually tells you how to catch a ghost," explained Evangeline.

"You can't catch something that doesn't exist," responded Giselle.

"I bet Ty would disagree," Evangeline said with a smirk. "Let's go ask him."

"No! Fine, we'll try it your way," Giselle said, before Evangeline could embarrass her.

"What about my beauty sleep?" whined Mercedes. "I can't stay up all night."

"Mercedes, the only way to truly make Emma feel safe is to catch the ghost," answered Evangeline.

Giselle could see Mercedes wasn't convinced. She didn't think they would actually catch the ghost, but she did like the idea of seeing Ty again tonight.

"We need your expert acting skills to pull this off," said Giselle, buttering her up.

Mercedes groaned. "Sometimes my talent is a curse."

Her sisters knew it was best just to nod and act like they agreed.

Ty motioned for the GEM Sisters to follow him to the other side of the stables. "Girls, ready to ride?" asked Ty, trying not to laugh. "Then come meet Cynthia!"

Mercedes had pulled out her phone ready to film. She gasped in disgust.

"Cynthia" wasn't a horse at all. She was an ugly gray Halloween costume. The costume was placed over a giant log to look like a real horse, but it was fake!

Giselle watched Ty's eyes sparkle as he laughed.

"First you gotta learn to mount the fake horse, then you can mount a real horse," said Ty.

"Aw poopsicles!" said Mercedes, disappointed.

"Who's first?" asked Ty.

Evangeline raised her hand, then sneezed. "Ah ah kamakazeeeeee! Nope that's not it."

The Sister Detectives had no clue how, but they knew one thing for sure. Tonight, they were going to catch the Ghost Horse!

CHAPTER 4

Mercedes was riding on a beautiful, white horse with large wings and a pink sparkly unicorn horn. The *Horse Divas'* film crew followed her every move. She controlled her magical horse with ease. Everyone was chanting, "We love you Mercedes!"

She felt an annoying tickle on her cheek. Was it a fly? Or a mosquito? She ignored it and smiled.

"I love you too!" Mercedes yelled to her adoring crowd.

The fly came back even angrier, this time biting her cheek. Ouch! She tried to smack the fly off her face and it caused her to fumble. Down, down she fell.

Evangeline tapped Mercedes on the cheek. "Wakey wakey princess!" she teased.

Mercedes woke up from her dream, unsure

of what was going on. She remembered that Miss Amy had called lights out several hours ago.

"Sssh!" ordered Giselle.

Mercedes saw that everyone in the cabin was asleep except for her sisters. Giselle pointed to Amy's empty bed. She wasn't there.

"Where's Miss Amy?" asked Mercedes.

"I don't know," answered Giselle. "Probably helping Ty get the horses ready for filming. Let's hurry, so we can get back before anyone knows we were gone."

The sisters quietly took off their pajamas revealing the dark outfits they were wearing underneath.

"You're right! That is a good tip," Giselle said to Evangeline.

"Thanks!" whispered Evangeline. "Hurry. Stuff your pj's in your sleeping bags so it looks like we're still in bed.

Mercedes grabbed her little mirror to check how she looked. It showed her making a disgusted face. These clothes were so drab and dark. Her sisters saw that familiar look in her eye. Hashtag fashion regret.

"No changing outfits!" Giselle and Evangeline said at the same time.

***

After a short walk in the chilly night air, the girls arrived at Graveyard Hill.

Evangeline was super excited to be there, "Feel the cold? It's just like my book says, the air gets colder around ghosts." She flipped through the pages of her book reading with her flashlight.

"Maybe this is too dangerous," said Mercedes trying to hide how frightened she was.

"Do you really think Mom and Dad would have us here at camp if they thought there was any actual danger?" asked Giselle.

Just then Giselle noticed that Mercedes had added a colorful pink scarf to her black outfit. "Where'd you get that scarf? We're supposed to blend in," ordered Giselle.

"I'll have you know the scarf was always part of the agreed upon outfit for tonight," lied Mercedes.

A low scary moan echoed across the field, "Uhmmm. Wooo Maaaammaaaaaaa."

The sisters froze.

"Oh my gosh! What is that?" worried Mercedes. "I'm not dressed for this type of drama."

"Shh!" whispered Giselle. "Listen."

The frightening voice grew louder. "Uhmmm. Uhmmm. Woooo Maaaammmaaaaa!"

"Cut!" yelled Mom. "Let's try the chant again but with a different angle. I want to see the moon glowing behind you."

The voice was Callahan filming for his TV show. Once again, he had on his cheesy red cape. GEM Sisters quietly watched their parents move the camera.

"Mom does not sound happy," said Mercedes.

"Nope," agreed Giselle. "But now, we know where they are, so we can avoid them."

Giselle didn't want to get grounded before camp was over. She needed every moment possible to spend with Ty, so they could fall madly in love. She glanced at the horses grazing on the grass. Sadly there was no Ty.

Evangeline slammed her book shut, making her sisters jump.

"Okay let's catch this ghost! I just need a few more things for my plan to work," said Evangeline.

"Well let's hurry," said Giselle. "We don't know how much time we have."

The sisters quietly snuck into the stables near Graveyard Hill. They made sure no one was inside before they turned on their flashlights.

"Down here," motioned Evangeline.

All of the horses were outside grazing in the field, so it felt creepy and quiet inside the empty, dark stables.

Mercedes moved her flashlight on the ground. She almost stepped in a pile of poop. Phew! That was close. She held up her flashlight. Standing before her were two spooky eyes!

"Aaahhh! Ghost!" screamed Mercedes.

"Quiet!" ordered Giselle. "It's just a horse costume. Remember, you saw it earlier today?"

"Oh yeah," Mercedes said as she laughed nervously. She was a bit embarrassed she had screamed over a costume.

Evangeline showed her sisters the book about how to catch a ghost. She explained her plan was to have them dress up in the horse costume.

"I want to RIDE a horse, not BE a horse!" complained Mercedes.

Giselle held up the two person horse costume. "I think this will be great practice for your audition," joked Giselle. "You make a great horse booty."

"That's it! I'm going back to the cabin to get more beauty sleep," said Mercedes in a huff.

"Quiet, both of you!" commanded Evangeline.

Mercedes and Giselle weren't used to Evangeline barking orders. They waited quietly for what she was going to say next.

"Mercedes, you and I are going to wear the horse costume. I'll be the booty so stop complaining. We are all going to work together and help Emma by catching the ghost," instructed Evangeline.

She explained the plan to her sisters. "Mercedes and I will dress up as a horse and hang out on the field with the other horses eating grass. Then, when the Ghost Horse appears, we will chase him into the stable."

Mercedes raised her hand.

"No questions until the end," responded Evangeline.

She continued, "After we chase the Ghost Horse into the stable, Giselle will close the door and trap the ghost. Then, Giselle holds up this little mirror. The horse looks in it and BAM! He's trapped in the mirror forever. Easy peasy."

Both sisters' hands shot up. Evangeline pointed to Giselle.

"Why am I stuck in the stable with the Ghost Horse?" asked Giselle.

"Because you're the only one big enough to close the heavy stable door. Duh!" answered Evangeline. She pointed to Mercedes for her question.

"Just one issue. Is that my mirror?" said Mercedes upset. "I don't want a ghost trapped in there forever. The only face in that mirror, should be me!"

"That's your one problem with this plan?" Giselle asked, confused. "Ya know what? Never mind. Great plan Evangeline. Let's do it."

"Fine, you can use my mirror," said Mercedes, "but you're buying me another one if it gets haunted."

"So, what happens after I trap the light beam—I mean scary ghost—in the mirror?" mocked Giselle.

Evangeline put a concerned hand on Giselle's shoulder. "I really hope you take this seriously. But just in case you don't, it's mostly been nice being your sister."

"Why did you say that?" asked Mercedes.

"Because it will be too late when Giselle finally realizes I'm right. That the ghost is real. And then, the Ghost Horse will touch her and she'll be a ghost forever."

"Evangeline, you're so wise," said Mercedes. "Been nice knowing you Giselle."

"Would you two stop it?" ordered Giselle. "Just put on the horse costume so we can get this ridiculous plan over with."

The sisters worked together to put on the two person horse costume. It was a lot harder than it looked. At first, they didn't know where to put Evangeline's arms. It looked like the horse had six legs!

Eventually, Giselle realized how to fix it. Mercedes stood tall, wearing the front part of the horse costume. Then Evangeline put on the back end of the costume and wrapped her arms around Mercedes' waist. Evangeline leaned over, making her back flat, and placing her head by Mercedes' bottom.

"You better not fart!" Evangeline said seriously. She had no idea being the rear end of the horse costume meant her face would be stuck next to Mercedes' booty!

"No promises," giggled Mercedes.

Learning to walk like a horse was even more difficult than putting on the costume. Evangeline immediately took off at a faster pace than Mercedes. She bumped into her from behind, which knocked Mercedes off balance, causing them to trip and fall.

"We don't have time for this," said Giselle as she helped them up.

Mercedes and Evangeline worked out a system to help them walk to the field.

"Left foot. Right foot. Left foot. Right foot," repeated Mercedes, over and over, as they walked in sync.

Mercedes could see from her costume eye holes that they were getting closer to the large group of grazing horses. Luckily, Callahan had Mom and Dad distracted. So they didn't notice the fake horse sneak into the herd of real horses.

"Stop!" said Mercedes in a loud whisper.

Evangeline wasn't expecting Mercedes to stop without warning. Her face smooshed into Mercedes' booty. "Gross! A little warning next time," she mumbled.

Mercedes shushed her sister. They were standing close to the film crew. She was trying to listen to what Callahan was saying.

"Lick this," Callahan said as he held up a small twig to Mom's face.

"Sorry. I'm not a person who licks things where animals pee," replied Mom.

Dad felt he had to do what Callahan asked. He was paying them after all. So, he grabbed the twig and gave it a lick.

"It tastes like a dead dirty tree branch," said Dad, as he spit on the ground.

"Exactly! This has to be the spot. Ghosts love dead things and this twig belongs to a tree that has been dead for quite some time," explained Callahan.

Mom thought this made no sense at all. She looked away and rolled her eyes.

"Flooo-fla!" sneezed Evangeline.

"What was that?" asked Callahan. "Start the camera!"

Mercedes watched Dad point the camera directly toward them. Quickly, she put her horse head down so it looked like they were chomping on grass.

"Oh no!" whispered Evangeline. "I have to sneeze again."

"Hold it in!" ordered Mercedes. "You're going to blow our cover."

Evangeline wrinkled up her face as tight as

she could to hold in her sneeze.

Back by the stable, Giselle was watching, but she was too far away to hear anything. For a moment she feared her sisters had been spotted. Then Dad turned the camera back to Callahan.

"Greetings night owls," Callahan whispered into the camera. "It's the midnight hour and we are awaiting the arrival of the Ghost Horse. The darkened moon, hidden by the clouds, tells us that we are in for an animal haunting this very night."

As if on cue, a smoky mist crept along the field. Mercedes watched the smoke cover the grass and head towards them.

"Is this part of the show?" Mercedes said in a concerned voice.

"I can't see. Is what part of the show?" asked Evangeline.

Giselle watched the smoky mist fill the entire field. Suddenly, a powerful horse cry rang out. The sound of thundering horse hooves hitting the ground echoed across Graveyard Hill.

Mercedes watched as the horses' eyes grew wide. Within moments, the horses were kicking up their hooves and starting to scatter.

"Move back!" Callahan shouted to Mom and Dad.

"Evangeline run!" screamed Mercedes.

As fast as they could, the girls ran together. Left! Right! Left! Right! They were so focused on their feet, Mercedes didn't notice they were running straight toward Dad.

CRASH!

The girls knocked Dad to the ground and tumbled on top of him. Quickly, they scrambled to their feet and kept running. The herd of horses was right behind them.

Dad rolled out of the way before he was trampled. His camera wasn't so lucky.

Giselle ran in front of the stable doors. "This way! Over here!" she yelled, motioning to her sisters.

That's when she saw it. Through the smoky mist, a white glowing horse burst out from the middle of the herd. It was headed straight for them.

Giselle screamed to her sisters, "Faster! It's behind you!"

Mercedes didn't look back. She and Evangeline could barely breathe. They ran faster than ever before. Left! Right! Left! Right! Left! Right!

Giselle rushed over to the stable door and started to close it. Mercedes and Evangeline were almost there, but so was the Ghost Horse.

In a flash, her sisters fell inside. Giselle shut the door with all her might.

SLAM!

Safely inside, the girls fell to the ground. Their hearts wouldn't stop pounding.

"I can't believe it," gasped Giselle. "The Ghost Horse . . . *is real!*"

CHAPTER 5

"Lookout!" shouted Miss Amy.

An arrow flew high in the air. The girl campers took cover. The arrow seemed like it was coming straight at them, but then it curved and landed nowhere near the archery targets.

Miss Amy grabbed the bow out of Giselle's hands.

"Sorry," yawned Giselle. "I don't know why I'm so tired today."

Giselle was lying to Miss Amy. She knew exactly why she was tired. In fact, it was all she could think about. She had literally seen the Ghost Horse last night. Her eyes had to be playing tricks on her.

Miss Amy handed the bow to Evangeline, who was next in line. "Your turn."

"No thanks," replied Evangeline. "I don't believe in violence. Unless of course it's a video game. Then watch out!" She did a karate kick in the air.

"Can I go next? I love archery!" said Emma as she took the bow. She made a serious face, and aimed the arrow at the target. *SMACK!* It hit the bullseye.

Everyone cheered for Emma. Everyone but Mercedes who was missing from the group.

Evangeline turned to Giselle and whispered, "Told ya it wasn't a light beam. Since you lost the bet, I thought I would be nice and let you choose the color of your shirt."

"I didn't lose," whispered Giselle. "I still don't know for sure if what I saw was a ghost."

"Shhh!" said Evangeline. "Keep the ghost talk down or else Emma is going to hear you. We don't want to scare her again. Look how much fun she's having."

Evangeline was right. Emma didn't know that they were being Sister Detectives, working to solve the mystery. Why have her worry until they knew more?

Mercedes walked up, filming herself on her phone. "Good morning GEMS! I hope you're having an amazing day. We're having the best time at horse camp!"

Mercedes turned the camera to face Giselle

and Evangeline. They said "we love you" at the same time, then blew kisses at the phone.

"And post," said Mercedes with a smile. She tucked the phone back into her jean's pocket.

"Mercedes!" called out Miss Amy. "Glad you could finally join us. That was the longest trip to the bathroom that anyone has ever taken in the history of this camp."

"You can't rush perfection!" said Mercedes with a smile.

Miss Amy asked Emma to show the other campers how to properly hold the bow. This left the GEM Sisters alone to talk.

"So what did you find out from Mom and Dad," asked Giselle.

"It was horrifying!" said Mercedes dramatically. "My phone was down to 36 percent. But don't worry, Dad found me a portable charger." She held up the black cable plugged into her phone.

"About last night!" ordered Giselle. "You were supposed to go find out if they filmed you two in the horse costume."

"Oh, Dad totally did," answered Mercedes. "But the good news is his camera got destroyed by horses so they don't have any footage."

"Anything else?" asked Giselle. "Did they

mention actually seeing the Ghost Horse?"

"No, but I found out they are planning to film again tonight," explained Mercedes. "Mom was all like, 'this whole thing is so dumb'. And Dad was like, 'how can I film without my special night vision camera'. And blah blah blah!"

"That's a really good Dad impression," said Evangeline.

"For once, can you two focus on what is important?" begged Giselle.

"Yes!" Mercedes answered. "My phone is at 68 percent!"

Giselle rolled her eyes. Sometimes she didn't know why she even bothered.

"Let's go talk to the chief. He knows everything there is to know about the Ghost Horse," explained Giselle. "We need to get out of here. Any ideas?"

Evangeline turned to Mercedes. "Quick. Fake that you're hurt. You know, like you do at home when it's your turn to unload the dishwasher."

"I never fake," started Mercedes. She stopped in her lie. It was pointless. Her sisters knew her better than anyone.

Mercedes motioned for her sisters to

stand back. "Get ready for an award winning performance," she said with a smile.

"Aaaah," screamed Mercedes as she dropped to the ground. Tears filled her eyes as she held her arm. "I got stung by a bee! It hurts so bad! Ow!"

Miss Amy ran over to Mercedes. "Are you okay? Are you allergic? Let me see."

Mercedes held out her arm, but Miss Amy didn't see any red bumps. Quickly Mercedes pulled her arm back and held it tightly.

"I just want a Band-aid," cried Mercedes.

Miss Amy felt that Mercedes was overreacting, but could tell that she wasn't going to stop crying until she got a Band-aid. She turned to Giselle and Evangeline.

"Please take your sister to the main office. Ask the chief for a Band-aid," said Miss Amy. "But hurry back!"

Mercedes continued to whimper as the GEM Sisters walked away. She instantly stopped once they were out of eye sight from Miss Amy.

"You gotta teach me how to do that," said Giselle.

"Sorry, an actress never reveals her secrets," answered Mercedes with a flip of her hair.

***

After a short walk, the girls arrived at the main camp office. Once inside, they couldn't believe how cluttered it was.

"Look at all this cool stuff!" said Evangeline excitedly.

Back home Mercedes and Evangeline shared a room, so Mercedes was used to her sisters' mess. The chief's office, however, took being a packrat to a whole new level.

The office looked like a really messy museum. Native American objects covered the floor and walls. There were brightly decorated baskets and rugs, plus lots of jewelry and clothes. A large carved totem pole leaned against a wall filled with framed pictures.

"Hello, young warriors," said the chief from behind his desk. He was surrounded by papers. Water dripped from a ceiling pipe into a bucket on his desk.

DRIP! DRIP! DRIP!

The elderly chief wore traditional Native American clothing. A tan shirt covered in fringe d colorful beads. His long gray hair was styled into two braids.

Mercedes was wearing the same braided hairstyle today. She almost said *totally twinning*, but then she remembered she was supposed to be acting hurt.

"Ow! I need a Band-aid," whined Mercedes holding her arm. "It has to be pink so it doesn't clash with my outfit."

The chief's face curled up, confused. His eyes followed her fingers to the invisible wound. He could tell she wasn't hurt. Still, he opened an expired box of tan band-aids and handed one over.

"Thanks?" complained Mercedes as she tried to put on the ugly Band-aid. It had lost all of its stickiness.

"Cool horse necklace," said Evangeline, pointing to the chief. "Is that for the Ghost Horse?"

"This is my spirit animal totem," he explained holding the necklace. "What you call ghosts, my people call spirits. We are given spirit animals to help and guide us."

The chief took off his necklace and handed it to Evangeline for a closer look.

"Every one of us has a spirit animal that

chooses us. Have you ever felt drawn to a certain animal, but don't understand why?" the chief asked Evangeline.

"Yes! Unicorns," Evangeline answered. "Sometimes I feel like I'm a unicorn in human form. I spread joy and smiles, and I poop rainbows!"

The chief chuckled. "What an interesting young one you are. I find that kids today do not believe in legends and spiritual things. But I do know why the Warrior Spirit Horse appears on Graveyard Hill."

Giselle tried to play it cool, but they didn't have much time. Miss Amy had told them to hurry back. She needed answers and the chief was a bit of a slow talker.

"So you really think the Ghost Horse is real?" asked Giselle.

"My people have shared the legend of the Warrior Spirit Horse for many moons," continued the chief. "We were told stories around the campfire as children. We then passed on those stories to our own children and grandchildren."

The chief paused for a moment then started slowly talking again.

"We chose to honor the burial grounds with

this camp. It has kept my people's culture alive. Activities like horseback riding, archery, crafting, and even the campfire stories. It's all done to honor us and our legends. And now the spirit horse honors us back by—"

"Why do you think the Ghost Horse is showing up now?" asked Giselle before he finished telling his story.

Giselle was getting frustrated. She wanted 'yes' or 'no' answers, but every answer the chief gave sounded like a long riddle.

"I have felt its presence more this week than ever before. The Warrior Spirit Horse is sending us a message. Now is the time we should be still and listen. He has awoken to protect this land. He is looking for a new rider to help him."

Giselle shook her head and disagreed. "So, if the Ghost Horse is real, which I'm not saying it is, then all the campers here are in danger."

"Danger? No. Everyone here has the honor of becoming the Warrior Spirit Horse's new rider. I only hope that he chooses me," said the chief as he stood.

"So, you want to be turned into a ghost?" asked Evangeline. "That's so cool."

Giselle absolutely did not think it was cool.

In fact, this was the craziest thing she had ever heard. Who would want to be turned into a ghost?

Mercedes responded, "Ew! I don't want to be turned into a ghost! I mean, it might make me famous. But no! I would barely show up in selfies because I'd be all see-through-ish. Plus, I could never be on *Horse Divas* if I'm a ghost!"

"What's a horse divas?" asked the chief.

"It's this amazing TV show about a group of fashionista girls who enter competitions and ride horses! I'm auditioning for it," explained Mercedes.

"I don't watch TV," said the chief. "All of this new technology mumbo jumbo clutters the mind. It distracts from the old ways."

Giselle looked at all the junk in his office. Clearly, the chief had no problem with his own type of clutter.

The chief walked over to the wall of frames next to the large totem pole. He examined the photos and then took a frame off the wall.

"My grandchildren, Ty and Amy," he said as he handed the frame to Giselle. "They used to perform in horse competitions."

The picture was of Ty standing inside a horse stadium. He was holding a large trophy.

Giselle sighed at his cute smile.

"Those two have always shared a deep connection to horses. They won lots of awards back in those days. But now Amy is too busy running the camp to ride, and Ty only seems to have time to train horses."

"I bet it's also hard for him to find time for a girlfriend," said Giselle, hoping he was single.

Both Mercedes and Evangeline looked at Giselle and rolled their eyes. Giselle didn't care. The chief gave her the answer she hoped for. Ty was single as a Pringle.

Just then Mercedes spotted an old trophy in a pile of junk. She picked it up and started filming herself on her phone.

"This is just one of the many awards I've won for my expert riding skills," lied Mercedes. "I can't wait to bring my long list of riding talents to *Horse Divas* so the whole world can enjoy them."

Giselle grabbed the phone out of her hand. "You can't say that."

"It's my audition. I can say what I want," argued Mercedes. "Give me back my phone!"

"Do you see how the little electronic box brings about conflict?" asked the chief. "Let us settle our differences with words not…"

Before the chief could finish his long speech, Mercedes took back her phone, pulling back hard. The sudden jerk caused Giselle to drop the frame.

CRASH!

Glass smashed as the frame hit the ground. Giselle quickly bent over to pick it up, but her arm accidentally knocked over the bucket of water on the chief's desk.

SPLASH!

Water spilled all over his desk onto the piles of papers.

"Oh no!" cried out the chief. He ran to his desk. He quickly picked up papers and started shaking off the water.

The girls rushed over to help, when Amy entered.

"What's going on here?" she asked. "Grandpa, the girls are supposed to be at lunch. But since you don't have a phone, I had to walk all the way over here."

"A phone is what caused this unrest," the chief said sternly.

The girls worked quietly while the chief and Miss Amy argued. Mercedes used a towel to clean up the water. Giselle set the papers by the window to dry in the sun. Some were old camp flyers, and some were hand drawn pictures from campers. Others were bills for the camp with the words "Late Fee" and "Must Pay Now" stamped on them.

"There are lessons to be learned from nature. The new ways aren't always the answer," lectured the chief.

"Not now grandpa," complained Miss Amy. She picked up the bucket and put it back under the ceiling's leaky pipe. "Girls, go to the cafeteria. And hurry, or else you're going to miss lunch!" she ordered.

"GEM Sisters," said the chief, "may the Warrior Spirit Horse guide your ways and your time at this camp."

Miss Amy groaned upon hearing about the Ghost Horse. She decided not to argue, and instead went back to cleaning up the mess.

The girls walked together on the dirt path to the cafeteria.

Mercedes took the non-sticky Band-aid off her arm and tossed it in the trash. "Now what?" she asked.

"Well, we learned that this mystery is more serious than we thought," explained Giselle. "The chief believes the Ghost Horse is real. If he's right, then all the campers are in danger."

Evangeline spoke in a serious voice, "Then it's time for us to be detectives. We have to stop the Ghost Horse before it comes back tonight!"

The Sister Detectives didn't know what to do next. But they had to figure it out soon, before one of the campers became a ghost . . . FOREVER!

CHAPTER 6

The GEM Sisters wished they would have walked slower when they saw what was being served for lunch. They weren't sure what they were looking at. In front of them was a mushy blob of orange-colored slime. Evangeline thought for sure it was some type of rice. Giselle insisted it was overcooked mac and cheese.

Mercedes poked at the gross goo with her fork. "I know what it is," she declared. "Garbage!" She tossed the food into the trash. "Another case closed!"

The crowded cafeteria was buzzing. Restless campers waited to hear their next activity. One cabin was released for the obstacle course, one for horseback riding, and another to go swimming in the lake.

The GEM Sisters' cabin was given the arts

and crafts station. Evangeline was thrilled, but Mercedes and Giselle . . . not so much. They both wanted to go horseback riding, but for very different reasons.

***

The campers walked into a dull looking tent. They were all surprised when they saw an art studio filled with colorful paintings, straw baskets, and tie-dyed shirts. There were tables covered with art supplies and white paper plates.

An older woman wearing glasses with long, straight, black hair stood at the front. She wore a blue apron covered in splatters of glue and paint.

"My name is Aponi. It means butterfly," said the art teacher. "Today we are going to be making animal masks. These will be your spirit animals for the campfire ceremony tonight."

"Can I make a unicorn?" asked Evangeline excitedly.

"Sorry, but in nature, no one gets to choose their spirit animal," explained the teacher. "Each of you will take a picture from this basket. Let the spirits guide your hand to find your match."

The girls took turns reaching into the basket. Trudy pulled out a picture of a brown bear. Emma chose a turtle. Mercedes smiled at her picture of a beautiful butterfly. And everyone laughed when Giselle pulled out a skunk.

Evangeline was last. She was not thrilled when she got a wolf.

"The wolf is a protector. It's an animal that can break away from the pack," explained the teacher. "From the look of your wild clothes, I'd say you definitely march to the beat of your own drum."

Evangeline liked what she heard. She decided to make her wolf mask with her own special touch. Rainbow ears.

The girls made masks while the teacher taught them a lesson about how Native American people respect animals. "We honor them by wearing feathers and animal totems. And by painting animals on our belongings," she told the campers.

Giselle raised her hand to ask a question. She wanted to ask about the horse totem necklace that the chief wore, but Miss Amy entered.

"Ladies, it's time for your next activity: horseback riding," Miss Amy happily announced.

All the girls cheered. They added final touches of glitter glue and beads to their masks.

"Please leave your mask on the table to dry," said the teacher. "I will bring them to the ceremony. Each of you should practice acting like your spirit animal before tonight."

"I think Giselle is practicing being a skunk right now," Mercedes said holding her nose.

"What? I didn't fart!" pleaded Giselle. "That smell isn't me."

The girls all giggled as they rushed out of the studio.

"I'll get you back for that," Giselle said to Mercedes.

"We'll see," responded Mercedes with a sneaky smile.

The campers walked on the dirt path that led to the stables. The GEM Sisters were together in the back of the group. They talked quietly so the other girls couldn't hear.

"What are we going to do to stop the Ghost Horse?" asked Evangeline. "We're running out of time. The sun will be setting soon."

The sisters realized they'd been having so much fun at camp they had forgotten to work on the mystery.

"Sometimes I think we're not very good detectives," realized Mercedes.

"This isn't like a normal mystery to solve," complained Giselle. "There aren't any clues to look for. It's not like a case where we're trying to find something lost or stolen. We're not ghost experts!"

"Greetings GEM Sisters," came Callahan's voice from behind them.

Not this guy again, the girls all thought to themselves. *At least he wasn't wearing his lame cape.*

"Your parents are getting some rest before we start another long night of filming. It seems they aren't quite night owls yet, but I'll get them there," he said.

"Doubt it," replied Evangeline. "Our dad loves sleep more than us."

"I hear you guys are famous like me," said Callahan. "Maybe I could be a special guest in one of your videos."

Mercedes held in her snicker. There was no way she was doing a video with this cheeseball. Hashtag cringey.

"Hey you're a ghost expert. Can you settle a bet for us?" Evangeline asked Callahan. "I read that the only way to stop a ghost is to have it look in a mirror. Then it will be trapped in there forever."

Callahan laughed out loud. "You kids have been watching too many comic book movies. The only way to stop a ghost is to—"

"Absolutely not!" Miss Amy shouted at Ty.

The girls had arrived at the stables to find Miss Amy and Ty in a loud argument.

"It's just a joke, Amy. Lighten up," replied Ty.

"The Forbidden Trail is no joking matter. It's dangerous and none of these campers are at expert riding level," she argued. "Stop telling the campers they should go on it."

"Forbidden Trail?" asked Callahan.

Ty noticed Callahan and ran over to give him a high five. "Oh, hey man! Yeah it's so cool. Like the ultimate adventure. Poison ivy, rattlesnakes, deadly spiders, and all kinds of scary creatures."

The look on all the campers' faces showed they did not agree. They thought the Forbidden Trail sounded terrifying.

"And the trail has dangerous drop-offs,"

added Miss Amy, annoyed.

"It's not that dangerous. I go up there all the time," explained Ty. He leaned over to Callahan. "You just gotta know where the drop offs are, because otherwise . . . *SPLAT!*"

Ty did a motion with his hands that looked like he was falling off a cliff to the ground below. The girls gasped.

"Do not worry, young ones," said the chief, sitting on his horse. "We shall not travel on the Forbidden Trail. The forest is filled with many wonders. My people have always lived in harmony with nature, not in fear of it."

Callahan leaned over to Ty and whispered, "Can you show me the trail tomorrow?"

"Sure man!" Ty nodded yes. He gave Callahan a fist bump.

"Girls, line up so we can help you mount your horses," instructed Miss Amy.

Giselle whispered to her sisters, "What should we do? We need to hear what Callahan knows about getting rid of ghosts."

Her sisters knew she was right. Callahan was a cheeseball, but he was the only ghost expert they knew.

Evangeline got an idea. "Mr. Callahan," she said. "We'd be honored to interview you in one of our videos."

"We should film it now!" Giselle joined in. "Come with us on the ride. Our fans would love to hear stories about your show."

"They would?" asked Mercedes. She realized her sisters wanted her to lie. "They sure would. I think the video would get millions of views."

The word "millions" got Callahan's attention.

"Well, I only wish I had my cape," he said to the girls.

"Oh, I think it's better to look more natural for the interview," Giselle said, trying to keep a serious face.

It was settled. Callahan started to mount a horse when Miss Amy objected. She didn't want him on the trail ride. She was afraid his stories would scare more campers.

Chief Black Feather interrupted, "Join us Mr. Wilcox. I want you to hear the truth behind the spirits you seek."

Miss Amy groaned, but chose not to go against the chief. She looked at Callahan sternly and said, "Don't frighten my campers."

The GEM Sisters were the last to mount their horses.

Amy helped Mercedes onto hers. Within

seconds she had her phone out filming her audition.

Giselle was next and, for a moment, she thought she was dreaming. Ty reached out his hand for her to grab. His hand was so rough and strong. She focused so much on his hand touching hers, that she lost control of her foot. It slipped out of the stirrups. She started to fall.

Giselle cringed and got ready to hit the painful ground. But it never happened. Ty scooped her up, and held her like a princess. She swooned. Up close his smile was so perfect, and his arms were like a . . . a . . . a cloud—, but like a cloud with muscles. She couldn't explain it. She just wanted the moment to last forever.

"Hey, Prince Charming!" yelled out Evangeline. "A little help here."

Somehow, Evangeline was stuck hanging upside down on the horse's saddle. Ty rushed over and helped her up. Evangeline reached into her pockets. Thankfully, her candy had not fallen out.

Evangeline grabbed a gum ball and handed it to Ty. "A tip for your services."

Miss Amy informed the group that she

and Ty were going to set up for the campfire ceremony. She reminded everyone to go slow, to listen to the chief, and to stay off the Forbidden Trail.

Amy looked at Callahan when she said the last part. It was obvious to everyone that she didn't trust him.

The campers formed a line on their horses and followed the chief.

Ty called out to them as they rode off into the forest, "Have fun exercising your horses. When you get back, it's gonna be s'mores, hot dogs, and an awesome campfire!"

***

The forest was beautiful and quiet. The campers felt like they were in a movie. They watched the sun set over the hills. A falcon soared above them. There were giant trees and the sky looked like a perfect painted picture.

The chief spoke with great authority, "My ancestors lived off of these woods. See that fresh animal poop? It helps grow crops. Everything on the Earth has purpose."

The chief described every weed and creature they rode by. His voice trailed off into a deep mumble. The campers tuned him out and admired the wonders of the forest.

At the back of the line of horses, the Sister Detectives were dealing with their own long-winded stories. Callahan hadn't stopped talking since the ride started.

"So, in *Animal Hauntings* episode 35, there was a ghost I called the Alabama Hamsta!" explained Callahan. "Every night at 3 AM you could hear the ghost hamster running in his squeaky wheel. The spooky sound filled the house. *Squeak. Squeak. Squeak.*"

Is this guy going to tell us about every single episode? thought Mercedes, annoyed.

Her face couldn't hide that she was frustrated. She needed to film her audition before the trail ride ended. "Oh no! I'm almost out of battery. Guess we'll have to finish the video later," she lied as she stopped filming.

"Good thing you have a portable charger in your pocket," said Giselle, not letting her off that easy.

Mercedes plugged the charger into the phone and glared at Giselle.

"Thanks big sister," said Mercedes with gritted teeth.

"Now, where was I," asked Callahan. "Oh,

yes, episode 36. The freakish goldfish. You see this grandma had accidentally flushed her pet goldfish and—"

"Ah ca cha mini poop!" sneezed Evangeline.

Callahan looked at her oddly. "Are you okay?"

Evangeline couldn't reply as she began a series of sneezes. "Ooo pooo sha! Ka la ma zooo! Aaah choo choo mah!"

Callahan turned to Giselle. "Is your sister okay?"

Giselle sighed. "She's fine. She's trying to invent the perfect sneeze."

Evangeline added, "Yeah, for some reason nature makes me sneeze a lot. So, it's a great place to work on my creation. Ahhh smoofie!" she sneezed again. "Nope, that's not it."

Giselle didn't know how much time they had left riding horses. They still didn't have the answers they needed. "You're clearly the expert in animal ghosts. Can you tell us how to stop a ghost? Ya know, like, make it leave for good?" asked Giselle.

"That's easy," bragged Callahan. "You have to help it with its unfinished business."

"Unfinished?" asked Mercedes. "Like when I don't finish cleaning my room?"

"Not exactly," he answered. "Ghosts stay behind because there is something they still want to do. If you help the ghost find what it is looking for, then it will leave."

"So, what does the Ghost Horse want?" asked Evangeline.

"Maybe he's looking for a new rider. Maybe he wants his old rider," explained Callahan.

"Like what? His bones?" wondered Giselle. "Is that why he keeps showing up on Graveyard Hill. To find where his rider's buried?"

"That's my guess," replied Callahan. "A lot of times animal ghosts are just wanting to have something that is special to them. A totem from their owner. Then they peacefully return to the ghost world."

"Ew! I'm out. I don't want to see creepy bones!" screeched Mercedes. She turned the camera on herself. "Hey! Mercedes here with another reason why you should pick me for Horse Divas!"

Mercedes swerved on her horse, trying to film while riding. She accidentally bumped into Trudy's horse in front of her. "Sorry!" called out Mercedes

"I'm fine!" said Trudy. "But ya'll are riding that horse like a rodeo clown."

"I can help you film," said Emma from up ahead. She slowed down her horse until Mercedes caught up to her in the line.

"Thanks for being such a great friend," smiled Mercedes. She stretched out her arm to hand her phone to Emma.

Together, they filmed several shots. Mercedes laughed. She acted serious. She lied about how she was a natural born rider.

"I got an idea!" said Emma. "I'll ride up ahead, then get a nice shot of you riding down the path."

"That will look great," agreed Mercedes. "Just yell action when you're ready."

Moments passed. She practiced different poses. Mercedes wondered what was taking so long.

"AAAAHHHH!!!!" a scream rang out from up ahead.

"Help!" shouted Emma. "I see the Ghost Horse!"

CHAPTER 7

Mercedes ran inside the cabin. "Emma wait!" she yelled.

Emma had already packed up her bedding. She was now stuffing things into her suitcase as quickly as she could. She was done with this horrible haunted camp.

"Miss Amy, you're sure she's coming tonight?" asked Emma, working her way towards the cabin door.

"Yes dear. Your mom said she's leaving right after work to come pick you up," answered Miss Amy. "It will still take her hours to get here."

Giselle and Evangeline could do nothing as Emma walked out the cabin door with Miss Amy. They were sad to see her go, but what could they do?

Mercedes couldn't just sit there. She ran outside and her sisters followed. She yanked on

Emma's suitcase to get her attention.

"Are you sure? Do you really have to leave?" asked Mercedes.

Emma stopped for just a moment. The beautiful swaying trees and quiet campground made the scary scene on the trail almost seem like it never happened.

"I'm sorry. I can't stay here anymore. I—I—I'm too scared," she whispered. "I'm waiting in the office and leaving the second my mom gets here."

"How is the office any safer?" asked Evangeline. "I'm just saying the Ghost Horse is supposed to only appear on Graveyard Hill. Now he's showing up in the forest. Who knows, the office might be his next stop."

"Evangeline, let's not make it worse!" added Giselle. "She's going home."

The GEM Sisters joined Miss Amy in walking Emma to the office.

Miss Amy did not like how Emma's mood was affecting the other campers. A bad mood travels fast, and she couldn't afford to lose any other girls.

"I know you think you saw a ghost, but I know for a fact that you didn't," explained Miss Amy. "My grandfather tells these stories that make your imagination run wild. But I've been at this camp my whole life. I promise, the Ghost Horse isn't real."

"But how can you be so sure?" asked Mercedes. "So many campers have seen it."

Miss Amy continued, "Every year campers supposedly see Bigfoot, or ghosts, or some type of swamp creature in the lake. But they're always just shadows, wooded animals, or faraway objects reflecting the moonlight."

Emma stopped and looked directly at Miss Amy. "I know what I saw."

They walked in sad silence the rest of the way to the camp office. Chief Black Feather was waiting by the door. The GEM Sisters gathered around Emma for a final group hug.

Giselle looked at Emma gently. "I think you're very brave. If you aren't having fun, then this is the right choice for you."

Evangeline pulled out a treat from her pocket and added, "But we will miss you! Here, have some lollipops for the road."

"Thanks GEM Sisters. You guys are so special to me. I will remember our good times together," said Emma. "Oh, and Mercedes I almost forgot. Here's your phone."

With all the Ghost Horse drama, Mercedes

had forgotten that she had given her phone to Emma.

Fewf, thought Mercedes. *That was a close one.*

"I hope my filming helps you get on the *Horse Divas* show!" said Emma.

"Awww thanks!" said Mercedes, feeling happy and sad at the same time. Mercedes gave her one last big hug. "Message me on social media so we can stay friends!"

Emma tried to speak, but she was too emotional. She quickly turned and walked into the office, holding back her tears.

Miss Amy and the GEM Sisters started the long, sad walk back to the cabin. They only went a few steps when Callahan stepped in their path.

"Greetings night owls!" said Callahan in his spooky TV host voice.

Mom and Dad were right behind him filming. They looked like they had just woken up. Dad was rocking some seriously hilarious bedhead.

Miss Amy put her hand over the microphone. "I'm *not* in the mood to deal with you right now. We just lost a camper."

Callahan shoved the microphone back in

her face. "You're responsible for this camp. The Ghost Horse was spotted again today. Is that upsetting you at all?"

Miss Amy didn't respond. She tried to turn and leave, but Callahan didn't give up. He knew how to push to get his story. He asked questions as fast as he could.

"Why do you think the horse was seen in the woods and *not* Graveyard Hill?"

"No comment."

"Do you think the ghost has already chosen its next victim? I mean rider?"

"No comment."

"Are you still having the campfire ceremony? Do you think the Ghost Horse will appear? Do you even care that one of your campers might be turned into a ghost forever?"

"You want the truth? Here it is!" shouted Miss Amy. "I feel like I can't win! We have new campers signing up because they are excited to see the Ghost Horse. But then, we have other campers leaving because of it! I just want campers to come and enjoy being at camp. I'd like the camp to be newer and not so run down. But, I never get what I want."

Everyone was shocked that Miss Amy had yelled at Callahan. That is, everyone except

Callahan. He had gotten Amy to blow up on camera exactly like he wanted.

"One last question. Are you finally a believer in the Ghost Horse?" he asked.

Miss Amy grew more angry. "Isn't it your job to make people believe? How's that going for you? Any footage of the ghost yet?"

Callahan made a cut motion for Dad to stop the camera. Mom took the microphone. The GEM Sisters listened as Callahan's face turned serious as he spoke to Miss Amy.

"I know you don't like me being here. But, if you want the camp to get paid the reward money, I have to film the Ghost Horse on video," explained Callahan.

"The Ghost Horse doesn't exist. However, a deal's a deal," said Miss Amy. "You can film tonight's ceremony *if* you stay put, by the fence, at Graveyard Hill. Stay out of the campers' fun. I mean it!"

Callahan saw no point in questioning Miss Amy anymore. He motioned for Mom and Dad to follow him to the fence where Amy pointed. He grabbed the microphone from Mom and kept filming.

"Night owls, the sacred campfire ceremony is only hours away. Are we standing right where the Ghost Horse will strike next? Is the Ghost Horse a legend, or a lie? I'll take you with me to find out once and for all. Two hundred years in the making, and it all boils down to tonight's ceremony."

Giselle rolled her eyes. This Callahan was such a talker. She wondered how much of his *Animal Hauntings* show was talking, and how much was actual footage of ghosts.

Callahan kept talking, "We'll feature Chief Black Feather in a moment. He'll tell us his thoughts on the Ghost Horse. Will it choose a new rider? Will a camper be turned into a ghost . . . *forever?*"

Dad zoomed in the camera, getting a tight shot of Callahan's face.

"Can we roll that again," asked Callahan. "I forgot to do my evil laugh." He cleared his throat. ". . . Forever? Ha ha ha ha! Wait. Do you think I should say 'forever' with a high voice or a low voice. *For*EVER or FOR*ever*. No. I liked it better the first time."

Miss Amy turned to the GEM Sisters. "I'm sorry you had to see all of that. I just want you kids to feel safe and have fun. Let's go."

The girls started walking back to the cabin. This time Mom ran over and stopped them.

"Hey! Sorry," said Mom. "Miss Amy, I'm with you. I don't believe in any of this ghost stuff. But . . . just in case, we want our girls to be safe. So, we don't want them to attend tonight's campfire."

"But Mom, I love ghosts!" pleaded Evangeline. "This is probably my one chance in my whole life to see one."

Mercedes added, "And I saved my favorite outfit to wear tonight."

"The ceremony might be dangerous," explained Mom. "We can't be filming and looking over our shoulder trying to make sure you're okay. Your dad almost got trampled last night."

Giselle had been hoping to sit next to Ty at the campfire. But she took one look at Mom's serious face and knew. There was no changing her mind.

"Yes Mom," answered Giselle. "No campfire tonight."

"Thanks girls for understanding," said Mom as she hugged them. "Dad and I will make it up to you later."

Miss Amy did not like the trend that was happening. First, Emma was leaving, and now people were not attending important camp activities.

"If this is really something you feel strongly about, then fine," said Miss Amy to Mom.

Mom started to apologize to Miss Amy, but Dad interrupted. He asked her to help set up a shot. She blew a kiss goodbye to the girls.

"You can stay in the cabin. But please don't tell the other campers why. I don't want a panic for no reason," explained Miss Amy. "Now, if you'll excuse me, I have a camp to run."

***

Back at the cabin, the girls saw their once fun-and-full-of-friends cabin as a dull, dreary prison cell. They were stuck here, all by themselves, for tonight.

Mercedes sat quietly, brushing her hair. Giselle's eyes glazed over as she imagined Ty sitting on the log by the campfire with no one to talk to.

"I wanted to eat s'mores and wear my wolf mask. Ugh. This stinks!" complained Evangeline.

With all the campers now gone, the cabin was quiet and still. It was the exact opposite of the fun slumber party they had first walked into.

"Maybe Miss Amy is right," said Giselle. "Maybe Emma doesn't know what she saw. Maybe it was a deer or a tree?"

"Well, I know one thing: this is the worst night ever," said Evangeline, flopping onto her bed. She reached under the bed and grabbed her suitcase. A small cloud of dust blew into her face. "Ah choo!"

"What about your perfect sneeze?" asked Giselle.

"What's the point anymore? We failed," said Evangeline. She grabbed four lollipops and shoved them into her mouth all at once without even looking at the flavors.

"It's so sad to see Emma's empty mattress and know she's gone for good," said Giselle. "If only Ty were here to hold me. I bet he's such a good listener."

Mercedes seemed to be taking it the hardest. She had climbed up in her bunk and had turned away from them. She wasn't saying anything.

Giselle felt bad for her. She was worried that they might all start crying. Emma and Mercedes had grown so close over the last few days. Before Giselle could say anything,

Mercedes leaned her head over her bunk.

"Guys, I seriously think I have a shot at *Horse Divas*!" said Mercedes holding her phone. "Look at this footage! Emma did an amazing job on my audition."

Giselle and Evangeline looked at each other, shocked. "Mercedes!"

"What? I'm sad too, but that was like five minutes ago," said Mercedes. "You can't expect me to spend my whole night on it."

"Wait! I might have spoken too soon," said Mercedes watching her phone. "Hmmm. It looks like Emma kept the camera filming, and I'm *not in it*!"

The chief's voice could be heard in the video. "We are the caretakers of Mother Earth. As the people of the land, we should never take more than we need, and we should use all that we have."

Mercedes scrolled impatiently through Chief Black Feather's speech.

"Maybe it's my fault. I should've taught her more about filming. But there was so little time," whined Mercedes. "Rule number one. Always keep the camera on *me*!"

"Give me that," yelled Giselle, as she snatched the phone from Mercedes' hands.

"I am so sick of you taking my phone!" shouted Mercedes. "Give it back!" she screamed, as she threw a pillow at Giselle.

"Quiet! Listen!" commanded Giselle.

She hit play on the video. The chief continued talking as Emma filmed different parts of the forest. She turned the camera to show the "Forbidden Trail" sign. Then, she tilted the camera up toward the top of the hill.

"*AAAAHHH!*" screamed Emma from behind the camera.

Giselle pressed pause. On screen was the Ghost Horse. It was a perfect shot. The scary, white Ghost Horse rearing up on its hind legs.

"That's the proof we need. Let's take this to Mom and Dad," squealed Mercedes.

Evangeline pulled the lollipops out of her mouth. "That still won't stop Emma from leaving."

She was right. They couldn't just prove the Ghost Horse was real. They had to stop the Ghost Horse by helping it with its unfinished business. But how?

Giselle scrolled back the video. She watched it over and over.

"Um. What are you doing?" asked Evangeline.

"Shhh!" ordered Giselle.

Evangeline decided to go back to her pity party. She put the glob of lollipops back in her mouth.

"OMG! That's it," blurted out Giselle.

Giselle paused the video on a close up of the chief. She zoomed in to see his horse totem necklace.

Evangeline and Mercedes looked at the screen, then at each other confused.

"I know why the Ghost Horse was in the forest," said Giselle as she ran to the door. "Come on! I know how to stop it!"

CHAPTER 8

The Sister Detectives were halfway across
the camp before Mercedes realized she had
forgotten her portable charger.

"We have to go back!" begged Mercedes.

"There's no time," explained Giselle.

"I don't know where you're taking us Giselle,
but I should warn you," said Evangeline, "I'm
down to only one pocket of snacks."

"There's no time for snacks. There's no time
for chargers," said Giselle. "We have to hurry
if we're going to stop the Ghost Horse and help
Emma."

"Well I'm glad to be out of that sad cabin,"
said Mercedes.

Giselle stopped outside of the camp's creepy
supply shed. It was old and rusty and looked
like a family of raccoons lived there.

"Never mind. This is way worse than the

cabin!" complained Mercedes.

"Guys, Callahan may be strange, but he's not crazy!" responded Giselle. She held up Mercedes' phone and paused the video. The Ghost Horse stood at the top of the hill. "We're going there."

"To the scariest place on Earth?" whimpered Mercedes. "Maybe Callahan isn't crazy, but you are!"

"No listen!" said Giselle. "Why is the Ghost Horse up there and not at Graveyard Hill?"

The girls looked at her speechless. Evangeline raised her hand.

"What are you doing?" asked Giselle. "You don't have to raise your hand."

Evangeline lowered her hand and answered, "Maybe he was there because he was running low on snacks?"

"What? No!" said Giselle annoyed. "And we're not going back for snacks."

Mercedes raised her hand.

"Or chargers," Giselle said sternly.

"Can we vote on this?" asked Evangeline.

"OMG!" complained Giselle. "I love you guys, but be quiet and listen!"

"Fine, smarty pants. You tell us. Why was the Ghost Horse there?" asked Mercedes.

"Because that is the final resting place of the fallen rider. Not Graveyard Hill," explained Giselle. "So all we have to do is dig it up, and the curse will be lifted!"

"You want us to be like grave robbers and dig up people's bones?" whined Mercedes.

"No, not bones," said Giselle. "This!"

She scrolled back the video on the phone. On the screen was Chief Black Feather. She zoomed into his horse necklace.

"I think the Ghost Horse is looking for the spirit totem of the fallen warrior. Just like how the chief wears his horse totem for his spirit animal.

"Phew! So no yucky bones," said Mercedes, relieved.

"Well the rider was probably buried with his totem," explained Giselle. "And bones buried in the dirt can last for hundreds of years, so . . ."

"Here's a better idea," interrupted Mercedes. "No gross woods. No creepy bones. We just steal the chief's necklace, and give it to the Ghost Horse. He's a ghost. He won't know the difference."

"We're detectives, we don't steal," said Giselle.

"Why not? It works," answered Mercedes.

"We're sticking with my plan," said Giselle. "Let's look for some supplies to borrow . . . not steal."

Inside the supply shed, the girls grabbed shovels of all different shapes and sizes. They weren't digging experts, so they didn't know exactly what they needed.

All of the shovels were old and mostly broken.

"No wonder this camp is so run down," said Mercedes "All of the tools are broken too!"

***

The sisters walked on the trail that led into the forest carrying their shovels and flashlights.

Unlike their horse ride during the day, the forest looked very different at night. The air felt heavy and smelled strange. There were constant spooky noises from the trees. Every step they took, it felt like creepy, yellow animal eyes were staring at them.

"Wait!" said Mercedes, stopping on the trail. "Mom said no leaving the cabin. I don't want to get in trouble. We should go back."

"We're already here," announced Giselle.

"And actually Mom said 'no campfire', so we aren't really breaking any rules."

Evangeline held up her flashlight to the wooden sign next to Giselle.

She read aloud, "This path contains hazardous drop-offs, dangerous snakes, poison oak and poison ivy. Cool!"

Mercedes pointed her flashlight on the sign, "The Forbidden Trail! Are you serious?" My phone battery is dying. My nails are nasty. I forbid *myself* from going on this trail. I am *DONE*!"

"Guys, it's the only way to stop the Ghost Horse. We can't chicken out now," begged Giselle.

"I'm *not* chickening out. I was born a chicken. Literally, if someone asked which came first the chicken or the egg, I would say me!" said Mercedes.

"Emma's not gone yet," reminded Giselle. "Don't you want her to stay?"

"Ugh! Fine. I'll be brave for Emma," replied Mercedes. "But if I die on this trail, you can be sure I'm coming back to haunt both of you."

The sisters walked in single file. First Giselle, then Mercedes, and last Evangeline. Their flashlights cut through the darkness like spears of light. Slashes of light went up and down as they walked.

Every now and then, one of them would yell, "Stop, poison ivy!" and "Careful, stay to the right."

Evangeline happily chatted away, "I was bummed to miss the campfire, but this is even better! Now I get to go on the Forbidden Trail, and see the Ghost Horse."

Mercedes burst through a spider web, and tried not to freak out. "Ew!" she squealed as she wiped the sticky webs on her pants. "No big deal. It's just a web. You're Mercedes. You can handle this."

Evangeline's eyes popped wide as she suddenly saw a big, black spider crawling up the back of Mercedes' shirt. She didn't want to scare Mercedes, but she could see its large eight legs creeping its way to her neck. Evangeline moved in closer to her sister and placed her finger next to the icky spider.

PING!

The spider, caught by surprise, went flying off Mercedes' shirt. "Phew!"

Mercedes spun around so quickly, Evangeline almost got whacked by her shovel.

"What are you doing?" asked Mercedes.

"Nothing," said Evangeline coolly. "There was a fluffy on your shirt."

"Oh. Thank you. Glad you saved me from that disaster," said Mercedes.

The sisters walked and walked and walked for what seemed like forever, but it was actually only ten minutes.

Giselle wondered what time it was. She looked back, and saw Mercedes checking her phone.

"What are you doing?" shouted Giselle.

"Chill out. I'm seeing how many likes my picture got today," replied Mercedes.

"I need you to save battery. That video on your phone is the only way we know where the Ghost Horse was standing. It's like our map," explained Giselle.

"Oops. I only have 25 percent battery left," said Mercedes.

Mercedes always complained about her phone battery. So Giselle knew 25 percent meant they only had a few minutes before the phone would die. Now, she secretly wished she had let Mercedes get her charger.

"Turn down your screen brightness," ordered Giselle. "And don't use the phone anymore until we get there."

The trees and sky had grown so dark around them. The girls were now walking at a faster pace. They had gotten used to avoiding poison ivy and spider webs. All of a sudden, Giselle put her hand out to stop her sisters.

"Wait!"

She pointed to the cliff drop-off. It was inches away from them. Perhaps Miss Amy was right. The Forbidden Trail was too dangerous. Giselle thought about what would happen if Mom found out this was all her idea. She would be grounded until she graduated college.

"Ya know what guys, you two should go back," said Giselle. "I can finish this case alone."

Giselle grabbed all of the shovels from her sisters. She tried balancing them in one hand and her flashlight in the other. She took one step, tripped on a tree root, and the tools came crashing down.

"You need us," said Evangeline. "We're the Sister Detectives. We're solving this mystery together."

"Evangeline's right. Besides, I don't trust you alone with my phone," said Mercedes with a smirk.

"Thanks guys. I guess when I was making

my plan, I should've known how dangerous this trail really is," said Giselle.

Evangeline grabbed her shovel and took off first. "C'mon guys."

A few steps later, a huge tree branch was in her way. She pushed the branch over, revealing a fork in the path. "Hey! Come check this out!"

"Well, this adventure just gets more difficult every minute," said Mercedes. "I'll let you guys decide which death path to take. But you might want to hurry, because my battery is at 10 percent."

Giselle looked both ways. She remembered in the video, the horse was standing next to a large pine tree. She started counting which trail had more pine trees.

Evangeline looked back and forth at both paths. She pointed left to right while she chanted, "My mom told me to pick the very best one and you are not it." Her finger pointed to the right side of the path. "We go left!"

"Works for me," said Mercedes.

Giselle started to explain the science behind why she had also chosen left.

"I don't need science," said Evangeline. "I've got luck."

The left trail didn't feel very lucky. They

found it very hard to walk on. The overgrown weeds were extra itchy, and it seemed like they were heading to a dead end.

The girls were about to turn back, when the weed covered path suddenly opened into a large clearing.

"Hey. It's the large pine tree from the video!" said Giselle excitedly. "Well, I think it is. I need to check the video to be sure."

Mercedes turned on her phone and gasped, "Only 3 percent. Hurry!"

Giselle grabbed the phone. In a panic, she opened the camera app, and quickly found the video. She pressed play and scrolled to the end where the Ghost Horse appeared. "Look!" she shouted.

The sisters all huddled around the phone. They stared at the screen where Giselle had zoomed in on the Ghost Horse by the tree. Then they examined the tree in front of them. They tried to compare the two trees when . . . the phone went *black*!

"Noooooo!" wailed Mercedes. "My baby!" She hugged the phone tightly.

"Now what?" asked Evangeline.

Giselle sat on the ground. She felt like crying. "We can't just dig somewhere. We need to know it's the right place."

Her sisters sat next to her and gave her a group hug. They sat in darkness, not sure what to do next. An eerie breeze came through. It caused the girls to shiver.

"It was a good plan," said Evangeline. "I mean it would have been better if it worked, but still it was good."

Another breeze came by, moving the clouds with it. The moonlight tried to poke through, but the clouds were thick.

"Well I'm willing to dig wherever you think we should," offered Evangeline.

"Why not?" added Mercedes. "My nail polish is already chipped."

Giselle smiled at her sisters' attempt to cheer her up. "Okay. Let's do it. Never hurts to try."

The girls picked up their shovels and walked to the tree Giselle had chosen.

The clouds drifted slightly. Then more, and more. Soon, bright moonlight filled the open area.

"Let's dig here!" said Giselle. "I'm pretty sure this is the tree."

"*What is that*?" asked Mercedes, scared by what she saw.

The moonlight revealed a spooky old barn just past the clearing. From where they stood, it looked like it was empty.

"Why is there a barn in the middle of nowhere?" wondered Giselle.

"Let's check it out," said Evangeline, already walking.

As the girls got closer, they heard strange noises coming from the barn. Something wasn't right.

Giselle shushed her sisters and quietly whispered, "There's something in there."

"Something like a bear?" Mercedes asked worriedly.

"Or like a ghost?" asked Evangeline.

THUD!

A loud bang came from inside the barn. The girls jumped. Something was definitely in there.

Mercedes stood, frozen with fear.

Giselle felt they needed to leave now. She motioned to Mercedes to quietly walk back to the path.

"Where's Evangeline?" whispered Giselle.

Both sisters' eyes darted to the barn. They watched as Evangeline crept inside the front door.

Giselle whisper yelled, "No! Evangeline!"

She was too late. Evangeline was inside.

"We have to go get her," said Giselle. Going back with only one sister was not an option. "Just stay behind me."

"Not a problem," answered Mercedes.

They carefully approached the barn. Mercedes held onto the back of Giselle's shirt. She was so afraid her hands were shaking.

Slowly, Giselle peeked inside the door. Evangeline was nowhere to be seen. All Giselle could see was darkness.

They crept inside, trying not to make a sound. Then, they froze. They heard something breathing. Mercedes closed her eyes. She didn't want to see what it was.

"Ah choo!" came a sneeze.

Oh thank goodness, thought Giselle. *It's Evangeline.*

"Ah choo! Ah ah ah choo! Ah choo! AH CHOO!" sneezed Evangeline.

Giselle could tell something was very wrong. Evangeline sounded like she was barely able to breathe.

Mercedes opened her eyes in panic. She was more worried about her sister than she was scared for herself.

They both frantically scanned the barn in

the low light, desperate to find their sister. Her sneezes bounced off the walls. Finally, Giselle found her.

Evangeline was hunched over, gasping for breath. She kept sneezing and sneezing and sneezing.

Then they saw something else . . .

It was the pale white Ghost Horse, with its nostrils flaring and its red flame eyes. Worst of all, it was right behind Evangeline!

Giselle and Mercedes screamed louder than they ever had in their entire lives.

CHAPTER 9

"Aaaaahhh!" The girls' long scream followed them as they ran out of the barn.

They ran as fast as their legs would move. Giselle spotted a large pine tree. She grabbed Mercedes and pulled her down. They both fell into the weeds behind the tree and hid.

They looked at each other, gasping for breath.

"Where's Evangeline?" asked Mercedes.

"I thought you had her," exclaimed Giselle. "She's still inside!"

"Oh no! She's a ghost for sure!"

"We are in so much trouble!"

"What do we do?"

"We don't know if she's a ghost yet," explained Giselle. "We have to go back and try to save her."

Giselle and Mercedes both looked at the

spooky barn. They were scared, but Evangeline needed them. Plus neither of them wanted to have to explain to their parents why they let her be turned into a ghost.

Slowly, they moved toward the barn, hiding in the shadows. They crept up to the door without making a sound.

"You peek inside," whispered Giselle.

"No, you," whispered back Mercedes.

"A *horse diva* wouldn't be scared!" said Giselle.

"I'm gonna die before I ever get to be a *horse diva*, thanks to you! You're the ghost hunter. You go first," Mercedes said as she pointed firmly to the door.

"Okay fine! But hold my hand," said Giselle. "I don't want us to get separated in there." She was frightened too, but she didn't want to say that to her little sister.

The girls held hands inside the barn. It was so dark they couldn't see anything.

"Evangeline," whispered Mercedes into the darkness. "Are you a ghost?"

"Shhh!" ordered Giselle. "Listen."

They moved in silence, feeling the dark walls of the barn to guide them. The sounds of the forest filled their ears. An army of crickets. A distant owl. A strong wind rustled the old barn walls. The noises all stopped at once. It was so quiet. Until . . .

CHOMP! CHOMP! CHOMP!

Mercedes panicked. "Oh my gosh! It's eating her soul. We're too late—"

Giselle tried to shush her, but Mercedes wouldn't stop nervously whispering.

"She's a goner! She's a ghost! Guess I'll have to turn her side of the room into a closet. Maybe I won't miss her as much if I have more clothes."

Giselle put her hand over Mercedes mouth to make her be quiet. A muffled, "Argh mmmph humph" still came out.

Mercedes eyes grew wide. She talked even faster, "Duh gooo herrrr!"

Giselle turned and saw the Ghost Horse. Her jaw dropped. Before she could scream, Mercedes used her hand to cover up Giselle's mouth.

Luckily they were behind the Ghost Horse and it was facing the other way. The sisters tiptoed back, still covering each other's mouths. They almost made it to the back door when . . .

CRASH!

Mercedes' phone fell out of her pocket,

landing hard on the ground. The Ghost Horse heard the sound and turned its head. He let out a powerful NEIGH! His eyes met hers. Mercedes was sure they were done for.

"Ah choo!" came a sneeze.

The ghost turned its head back to find the noise.

Evangeline, they both thought. *She's okay!*

But she wasn't. She was very much in danger. Evangeline was standing near the Ghost Horse's face. She just stood there, staring into the horse's eyes. Was she under the Ghost Horse's evil spell? She reached out to touch its face.

"Noooo!" yelled Giselle, leaping forward.

Giselle tried to grab her sister's hand, but it was too late. Evangeline touched the Ghost Horse. And . . . well . . . everything seemed to be okay.

"Oh, hey guys!" said Evangeline casually. "Ah choo!"

She reached out and petted the horse again on its large white face.

"Good boy. Sorry my sisters scared you. Ah choo!"

Giselle and Mercedes didn't know what to say.

"Guess what? I found out that I'm not allergic to nature. I'm allergic to horses!" said Evangeline happily.

Mercedes was finding her fear turning to anger. "I nearly wet my pants! And I dropped my phone." She checked her phone screen for cracks. Fewf! It was okay.

Giselle totally lost it. "That's what you learned, *Evangeline*? How about next time when we're totally freaking out, you yell something like, 'Hey guys come back! I found the Ghost Horse and by the way . . . *HE'S NOT A GHOST*!'"

"Okay. I'll try to remember that next time," said Evangeline. She fed the horse a big red apple.

CHOMP! CHOMP! CHOMP!

"Man this guy loves apples," said Evangeline, feeding him. She looked around for more.

"Sorry Marshmallow, that was the last one," Evangeline said. She reached into her pockets. "And I'm out of lollipops."

"Marshmallow?" exclaimed Mercedes.

"Yeah that's what I named him. Do you think Mom will let me keep him?"

"Wait? So this whole time the Ghost Horse

has been *fake*?" realized Mercedes.

"Looks like it," said Evangeline. She petted the horse's long hair and sneezed.

"Yes! That means, I won the bet!" cheered Giselle, doing a happy dance.

"You won, but only about this Ghost Horse," said Evangeline. "I still believe in ghosts."

"What's her shirt going to say?" asked Mercedes.

They all waited. And waited. It was obvious Giselle had still not come up with anything.

"Guys, right now the mystery is more important," lied Giselle.

"I wonder how the horse got all the way up here?" asked Mercedes.

"More like *WHO* brought the horse up here," added Giselle. "This whole time we have been trying to stop a ghost. When really, we needed to stop whoever is pretending to be a ghost."

Suddenly, they heard a stick snap outside in the woods.

CRACK!

The girls froze.

Giselle's face filled with worry. "Someone's coming," she whispered. "Quick! Hide!"

Giselle pointed to the stacks of hay in the corner. They ran and hid behind them, peeking through the cracks.

The girls watched as a figure, completely dressed in white, entered. The rider flipped a light switch by the door. Three large light fixtures, pointed right at the Ghost Horse, turned on. The light bounced off the horse and lit up the entire stable.

The girls weren't expecting such bright light. They covered their eyes in pain. One by one they squinted, slowly opening their eyes and getting used to the light.

Again, they peaked through cracks in the hay. The person was dressed in all white from head-to-toe, which included a white hood and white goggles to cover their face. The outfit blended in perfectly with the white color of the horse.

Mercedes couldn't help but wonder, *Is it an alien?* Then Mercedes noticed Evangeline's face start to crinkle up. She realized, *Oh no, Evangeline's going to sneeze*!

Evangeline pushed on her nose to stop her sneeze. But it was coming strong.

"Ah . . . Ah . . . Ahh . . . "

Their rustling caused the figure to look over toward the hay stacks. Giselle motioned for everyone to be still.

The person came closer, and closer. The more Evangeline fought the sneeze, the more it wanted to come out. They were inches from being discovered. The person started to lean over the hay when . . .

"Neigghh!" squealed Marshmallow, right as Evangeline sneezed.

"Ah cheeeeeeeeeee!" sneezed Evangeline, making a sound that blended in perfectly with the horse's neighing.

The person looked back at the horse. In a flash, the figure in white flipped off the lights, jumped on the white horse, and galloped away. Just like that, the girls found themselves safe but alone in the strange, dark barn.

"Wow, that was a close one," said Mercedes as she climbed out from behind the hay.

"Guys, this changes everything," realized Giselle. "We've been thinking about this mystery all wrong."

"Yeah, somebody is making people scared of Marshmallow. He's a nice horse. He doesn't want people to be afraid!" said Evangeline.

"And did you see their outfit?" asked Mercedes. "Wearing all white at a dirty horse camp? I don't think so. It was a huge mistake to bring my white leather boots because now they're totally filthy. There. I said it. I can admit when I'm wrong."

"We need to spread out and find clues," ordered Giselle. "Anything that can help us find out who that was."

Evangeline flipped on the lights. Before Giselle could say to turn them off, Mercedes screamed from the other room.

"Guys, get in here. I found something!" yelled Mercedes.

Giselle and Evangeline came running over.

"A phone charger. We're saved!" exclaimed Mercedes. She excitedly plugged in her phone. The phone turned on and beeped. She squealed.

Giselle realized that they were standing in a temporary office filled with clues. "Great job Mercedes!"

There were horse supplies everywhere, which was to be expected. But there were many other things that did not belong. Like a brand new tablet, buckets of white paint, and lots of boxes of different shapes and sizes.

Evangeline noticed a bucket full of apples. *Poor Marshmallow*, thought Evangeline. *He would have loved these.*

"Emergency over," said Mercedes. "I feel much better with my phone charging. Now I can focus."

"We need to solve this mystery fast. So I suggest we work together, discuss the clues, and make a list of suspects," said Giselle.

"Suh-what?" asked Mercedes.

"Suspects," explained Giselle. "The people we think might be the bad guy."

"Then just say possible bad guys," answered Mercedes. "It's easier to remember."

"We know the horse is being kept in this barn, but we also know that horses can't be left alone all day," said Giselle while she thought. "Remember, Ty taught us that horses are like humans. They need to be fed and exercised at the same times every day."

Mercedes whined, "And horses get to have people. People to style their hair, people who help them with their fitness goals, and people who win trophies for them. Why can't I have people?"

"Focus on finding clues!" ordered Giselle.

Evangeline found a tablet and handed it to Giselle. "Is this a clue?"

"Maybe," said Giselle, excited to see what kind of secret files or photos could be lurking inside it.

Giselle pushed the power button and it fired

up. Unfortunately, it was passcode protected.

"Rats!" Giselle sighed in disgust. "You just know the proof we need is in here. Oh well."

"Wait a second," said Mercedes. "You're giving up just like that? You keep going even when there's a trail of poison ivy, dangerous cliff drop-offs, and blood sucking snakes. You don't stop when a haunted barn holds a terrifying Ghost Horse, but you give up when there's a teeny tiny passcode problem?"

Mercedes grabbed the tablet. She held up her flashlight to the tablet screen. The screen reflected smudged fingerprints over the numbers where someone had touched it the most.

Giselle rolled her eyes. "Mercedes, the probability of finding the right four digit passcode is like 10,000 to 1. We'd literally be here all night before—"

"Ta-Da!" said Mercedes smugly. "We're in!"

Giselle's mouth gaped open. "What? How did . . .? What in the—"

"I've had plenty of practice at home with your guys' phones," bragged Mercedes. "Besides 1, 2, 3, 4 is a super common password."

Giselle made a mental note to change her phone passcode when she got back home.

Evangeline took the tablet and clicked on the video app.

"Oh wow, someone bought every episode of *Animal Hauntings*. Let's binge watch them all tonight!"

"How can you even see anything with all of this light glaring on the screen?" asked Giselle. She flipped the wall lights off.

That's when the sisters noticed drops of paint all over the ground. They were glowing!

"Of course!" said Giselle, realizing as she was saying it, "They're using glow-in-the-dark paint! The light bulbs charge the paint so that when the lights go off, everything that's painted white, glows!" She turned the lights back on.

"Oooh!" squealed Mercedes. "I found glow sticks! And here's a box for a smoke machine. A nice one with a remote control. I really want one of these for our next music video!"

"Hmmm," said Evangeline. "The *Animal Hauntings* show, this creepy barn, a smoke machine, and glow in the dark paint. I think we have all the proof we need. Case closed!"

"We did it!" said Mercedes giving Evangeline a high five.

Giselle was frustrated, "Seriously? Not even close. We found a bunch of stuff to prove

HOW the person makes the horse look like a ghost. We still don't know *WHO* is doing it. And *WHY*."

"Maybe the person doing this likes to scare people for fun," said Evangeline.

"I'm betting they're doing it for the reward money," added Mercedes.

"Could be. How much is the reward for Callahan's show?" asked Giselle.

Evangeline chose an episode of *Animal Hauntings* on the tablet and pressed play. Callahan appeared on the screen wearing his favorite red cape.

"Night owls, is there a ghost haunting you or a loved one? Contact us to be on our show. *Animal Hauntings* will pay $50,000 if your ghost is caught on camera! Watch out tonight for spooky dreams. Moo Ha Ha!"

Mercedes pressed pause on the video. "Told ya. It's always money sweeties."

"The late fee bills," remembered Giselle. "Chief Black Feather's desk was covered in unpaid bills for the camp. I bet that's what the money's for."

"Or it could be to buy a bunch of new stuff," explained Evangeline. "There are a lot of websites open on this tablet."

There were websites for skateboards, basketball hoops, and a new pool. Then, there were other websites for things like energy-saving light bulbs and water saving toilets.

The Sister Detectives didn't know what to make of all the random things they saw. Evangeline clicked on the last website that was open on the tablet. It was a site called 'Epic Pranks.' The page was filled with videos and "how to" instructions for pulling all types of pranks on people.

"Let's make a list of suspects. We will compare the clues and cross them off the list one by one," said Giselle. She picked up a pen and paper. "Callahan, Chief Black Feather, and Miss Amy." She wrote down the names one by one.

"Giselle, seriously?" asked Mercedes. "It's so obvious."

"Yeah, soooooo obvious," agreed Evangeline.

Evangeline and Mercedes looked at each other with a *should-I-tell-her-or-should-you* face?

"It's Ty!" shouted Mercedes and Evangeline at the same time.

"Noooooo! Not Ty. He's too cute to be the bad guy," whined Giselle.

"He loves *Animal Hauntings*. He knows how to take care of horses. He always goes on the Forbidden Trail. And he's an award-winning trick rider," explained Evangeline. "Plus, he was never around when Emma saw the Ghost Horse."

"And he's a prankster," added Mercedes. "He's probably going to buy all of that stuff to pull some huge prank on everyone at camp."

Giselle still couldn't believe it. There had to be a better suspect.

"You need more proof?" asked Evangeline. "Fine. Mercedes, play the video you made in Chief Black Feather's office. The one with the trophy."

Mercedes found the video and pressed play. The Sister Detectives all stared at the screen.

"This is just one of the many awards I've won for my expert riding skills," said Mercedes in the video.

Evangeline paused the video, showing the wall of frames behind Mercedes. The frames were filled with pictures of Ty and Amy holding awards. And standing next to Ty in one of the photos, was Marshmallow!

Giselle gasped. "Ty *is* the ghost rider."

CHAPTER 10

The GEM Sisters were tired and out of breath when they arrived at Graveyard Hill. The campfire ceremony had already started. There was a thundering of drums and chants in the air. And from what they could see, there weren't any s'mores left.

Mom and Dad were each setup in a different spot filming Callahan.

"Greetings night owls. This evening, we will finally witness the mysterious Ghost Horse. What you see now is a special ritual, meant to awaken the spirits of the netherworld. As per tradition, everyone is wearing their spirit animal costumes."

"The Ghost Horse hasn't come yet," realized Giselle. "We still have time to stop Ty."

Evangeline saw that everyone besides the film crew was wearing animal masks. She looked over by the campfire. There was a table with a few extra masks on it. "My rainbow wolf! Aww man. I practiced my wolf howl for nothing."

Since everyone had masks on, it was impossible to tell who was who. Chief Black Feather was obviously the tall person dressed as an eagle. His costume was very old. Standing next to him was a person with long, black hair dressed as a fox. It was most likely Miss Amy.

Callahan continued with great flare, "At the end of this ceremony, Chief Black Feather will perform the spirit animal dance. The dance will call to the Ghost Horse and it shall appear before our very eyes!"

Giselle explained to her sisters, "I know what Ty is doing. He's waiting for the dance. That way it seems more real."

"So? What's the plan to stop him?" asked Mercedes.

Giselle wasn't sure, but just then she noticed a hidden cord under the dirt. It wasn't like one of the video cables their parents normally used for filming. The cord was thin and ran along a row of bushes.

She motioned for her sisters to follow her. She scanned the ground to see where the cable led. They followed it to a large bush. As the sisters got closer, they heard a low buzzing noise.

"It's the smoke machine!" realized Giselle. "The machine is warming up. That means someone just turned it on and is about to use it."

"The smoke machine box in the barn had a picture of a remote on it," said Mercedes excitedly. "I bet that's how he starts the smoke."

"Then Ty has to be close," said Giselle. She looked out to the large field and over to the stables. She was trying to find something out of place. There was no sign of the Ghost Horse yet.

Evangeline glanced at Mercedes. She was glowing like a ghost.

"Oh no!" cried out Evangeline. "The chant is turning Mercedes into a ghost!"

"What?" asked Mercedes. "Aww man. My glow sticks must have turned on when I sat down."

"You stole glow sticks from the barn?" asked Giselle.

"Is it really stealing if you take it from a bad guy?" asked Mercedes.

"Yes!" both Giselle and Evangeline said at

the same time.

Giselle's eyes darted to the bright, white glow sticks, then to the stables, and then to the campfire. Her eyes went back to a fence that ran alongside the stables. There was a small, fenced in area with a metal gate.

"I've got an idea!" said Giselle. "But we don't have much time. Evangeline, I need you to create a distraction. Don't let the chief start the dance."

"How am I supposed to do that?" asked Evangeline.

"I don't know," replied Giselle. "Just be ready to have everyone look at that fenced in area." She pointed to the fence near the stables.

Giselle reached over to the smoke machine. She turned the setting from "medium smoke" to "high smoke".

"This should help," said Giselle. "Mercedes, come with me."

"Wait. Sister Detectives on three," said Mercedes. "One, two, three!"

With their hands together, they all whisper cheered, "Sister Detectives!"

"Be ready to close that gate!" Giselle yelled to Evangeline as she ran off.

Evangeline had several questions about the

plan, but her sisters had vanished.

Hmmm, she thought. *What would make a good distraction?*

Her eyes searched around the campfire. She locked onto the table with the leftover animal masks.

"Maybe I can have some fun and create a distraction at the same time," said Evangeline to herself.

Back at the campfire, Chief Black Feather spoke in a serious voice, "Young ones, we are gathered here to honor the animal spirits. Join hands to begin the dance my forefathers taught me. Let us summon the Warrior Spirit Horse together."

Just then, Evangeline burst through the crowd. She stood in front of the chief. She was dressed in her rainbow wolf mask, and waved for the campers' attention.

"My spirit animal is the wolf," she shouted. "I am the protector of this tribe. And I am here to make sure that the Ghost Horse does not hurt any campers."

Evangeline made eye contact with the chief, and quickly looked away. She did not want him knowing who she was.

"What do wolves do? We howl at the moon!"

she continued. "Let's hear you girls howl!"

The campers let out a huge collective howl. They were loving it and so was Evangeline. She led them in an even bigger howl.

"OWWWWW!"

"Thank you spirit wolf," said the chief, slightly annoyed. "Now be done. We must get back to the native dance and—"

"Do you doubt my courage?" interrupted Evangeline again. "I will battle anyone to keep this tribe safe!"

She noticed a camper in a bear mask sitting close by. The girl was wearing cowboy boots. It was Trudy! She turned to her.

"I do not fear even the most fiercest of creatures. I will battle this bear!"

Evangeline leaned over and whispered in Trudy's ear. "Trudy, it's me, Evangeline. I need you to pretend to fight me."

"Okay partner?" said Trudy confused. "If you say so."

The two girls stared into each other's eyes. They circled one another as the campers watched. This campfire ceremony was even better than they had expected.

Chief Black Feather stood awkwardly, not sure what to do.

"Roar!" said Trudy. She held her arms out like a bear and made scratching motions.

"Owwww!" howled Evangeline. She growled at Trudy like she was her worst enemy.

Meanwhile, Callahan didn't know exactly how to describe this part of the ceremony. "It appears this is the battle of the spirit animals, maybe?"

Callahan looked to Mom for the answer. She shrugged her shoulders with an *I-don't-know* face.

Mom stared at the wolf costume. She noticed the bright rainbow ears. She had a feeling that Evangeline was behind the mask, but she couldn't stop working now. Mom decided she would deal with her later.

Trudy roared louder! She jumped on Evangeline, accidentally knocking her down. The girls rolled on the ground pretend fighting. The fake battle went on for a while, until the chief's booming voice finally stopped them.

"Halt warriors! The spirits are saying it is time," ordered the chief. He pointed to the campers that sat in a small drum circle.

"Young ones," commanded the chief. "Begin playing the beat of the drums that free us all to dance."

The campers holding the drums began to play. People got up and started dancing to the rhythm. Evangeline tried one last time to stop the ceremony.

"Shouldn't we at least have a snack first?" asked Evangeline loudly. "You don't want to dance on an empty stomach do you?"

No one was listening. She looked over to the fenced in area, but there was no sign of her sisters. *Gulp.*

A mist of smoke trickled in and then filled in all around them. Evangeline was surprised that the campers hadn't really noticed. That is, until she saw they were paying attention to something else.

Across the field was a white, glowing object. The Ghost Horse was coming. Evangeline couldn't stop it now.

"Keep dancing," said the chief, "it's working!"

"It's the Ghost Horse!" someone screamed. The crowd was more amazed than scared. They couldn't believe the Ghost Horse was actually real.

"Remain calm and keep dancing," said the chief, leading the dance. "There is nothing to fear. He comes to honor us!"

"Night owls, as I live and breathe, I present to you . . . the Warrior Ghost Horse," said Callahan. "Captured on video, for the first time ever. It is both beautiful and frightening. I cannot look away!"

Callahan motioned for the cameras to zoom in on the horse, but his film crew couldn't see him, the horse, or anything else. Giselle had turned the smoke machine too high, creating a very thick fog. Callahan, Mom, and Dad all started coughing.

Dad kept trying to get the shot of the Ghost Horse. But it was too far away. With all the smoke, it just looked like a glowing blob.

A loud, far off voice shouted, "Everyone! There's a second Ghost Horse!"

Evangeline recognized the voice. It was Giselle. She glanced over to the fenced in area and saw another glowing horse. She squinted her eyes to see better. It was the gray horse Halloween costume covered in glow sticks.

Then she remembered the next step in the plan. "Everyone, look at the fence! It's a second Ghost Horse!" shouted Evangeline.

Callahan was the first to respond. "People, we have to move. Let's get away from all this smoke and get closer to the ghost. I want that

142

second ghost on camera right away. Go, go, go!" he ordered Mom and Dad.

The campers watched Callahan running. They all got up and sprinted after him. Evangeline panicked. This was *not* part of the plan.

"No! I didn't say go. I said look. Just use your eyeballs!" cried out Evangeline.

No one listened. Everyone ran, trying to get a better view.

Evangeline was the only one who noticed the first Ghost Horse picking up speed. He was coming straight for the crowd. She knew Ty wasn't going to miss this chance to be seen and get his reward money.

Evangeline took off running.

Mom and Dad also scrambled to follow Callahan in the smoky darkness. They were finding it very difficult to run, hold their cameras, film, and not bump into anything at the same time.

"Uh, oh," said Giselle worried.

"What's happening?" asked Mercedes. "I can't see anything back here."

Giselle and Mercedes were inside the horse costume. Giselle insisted on being in the front because she was taller, and oldest, and this was her plan.

"Well, everyone at camp is running straight at us," explained Giselle. "And I can't see the Ghost Horse because of all of the smoke I made. But I do see Mom and Dad. So, that's not good."

"Aaahhhhh!" screams cried out from the crowd.

"What was that?" said Mercedes, worried.

The sounds were getting closer, but Giselle couldn't see why.

Then, the crowd parted. She saw a very angry Ghost Horse racing toward them. It looked creepy, like it was galloping on air.

The Ghost Horse charged through the crowd and Giselle gulped. It was terrifying. She almost peed her pants. But she reminded herself, *No matter how scary it appeared, it wasn't a real ghost.*

"Hello?" whined Mercedes. "Can you tell me what is going on?!"

Giselle snapped out of her gaze. "Okay. Now the Ghost Horse is rushing toward us. Oh man. He's really coming fast. Quick! Move back!"

"Left. Right. Left. Right," the sisters said together as they backed away from the gate.

Giselle tried to see behind her so they wouldn't trip on anything. She was blinded by the bright glow sticks they had taped on the horse costume. She blinked her watery eyes, trying to focus.

As she turned her head around, the Ghost Horse charged through the gate. Within seconds, the Ghost Horse was running in fast circles around them, kicking up lots of dust.

SLAM!

Evangeline closed the gate, "Gotcha!"

Giselle glanced over. Evangeline was standing on the gate giving her a thumbs up.

"We did it!" Giselle told Mercedes.

The rider looked around and panicked. He realized he was now trapped. He yanked on the reins, causing the Ghost Horse to rear up on its hind legs.

The crowd surrounded the fence, trying to get a closer look.

The rider rode up to the fence, studying how high it was.

"Oh no! He's going to jump," realized Giselle. She looked around for a way to stop him. "Mercedes, what should we do?"

The crowd watched as the horse went from a fast trot to a full on gallop. He was rapidly picking up speed.

"If Ty gets away, we can't prove that he is

pretending to be the Ghost Horse," screamed Mercedes.

The rider let out a loud whistle, making the horse go faster.

This gave Evangeline an idea. "Spirit animals, howl at the moon!"

"Owwwww!!!!!" they all howled together.

The howls confused the horse, but only for a moment. The rider whistled loudly and snapped the horse's reins. The horse moved back into position.

The crowd now stood on the fence rails covering the entire fenced in area. There were people everywhere, except for one small section of the fence.

"I see where he's going to jump," said Giselle. "There's a small opening."

"I know what to do!" shouted Mercedes. "Get us over there."

"Left. Right. Left. Right," Giselle shouted as she kept her eye on the horse.

The rider started to charge toward the open area of the fence.

"Mercedes! We're almost there," said Giselle, quickly moving their legs back and forth together.

They made it to the opening. Now they were

blocking the Ghost Horse from escaping. The rider was moving at full speed straight at them. Giselle was getting nervous.

"He's going to jump over us . . . and the fence!" shouted Giselle.

"Not if we jump first," said Mercedes. "Get ready to jump as high as you can."

"Uh, Mercedes. He's going to hit us!" panicked Giselle.

"Wait for it, "said Mercedes. "One, two . . ."

The rider pulled back on the Ghost Horse's reins preparing to leap over them and the fence.

"Three!" she shouted. They both jumped high into the air.

The glow sticks caused a blinding light. The rider couldn't see where the opening was. In a panic, he pulled back on the reins, causing the horse to throw the rider off.

SLAM!

The ghost rider hit the ground. Everyone gasped.

Callahan burst through the gate. Mom and Dad followed closely behind him with cameras rolling.

"Night owls, we don't know what's going on yet. But I am going to find out," he said into the camera.

The rider moaned and stood up. The campers stared in shock. The figure in white scrambled towards the fence.

"He's escaping!" shouted Evangeline.

Giselle and Mercedes were stuck in the horse costume and had no way to grab him.

The Sister Detectives watched as the bad guy was about to get away. The rider was only a few steps from climbing the fence. Once he was gone, they would have no way of proving it was Ty.

At that moment, another horse and rider galloped through the gate. This rider had long black hair and was wearing a fox mask. The fox rider swung a rope high in the air. The lasso came spinning through the sky. It made its mark, and looped around the ghost rider before he could get away.

The crowd cheered.

The fox rider galloped in circles around the person in white. The rope got tighter and tighter until the ghost rider was completely tied up.

Callahan motioned to Mom and Dad to zoom in on the ghost rider.

"This rider is not a ghost, but rather, pretending to be one. I, Callahan Wilcox, will now unmask the person who has been lying to us all. Thank you brave hero for risking your life to expose this liar."

"Anything for you Mr. Wilcox," said a familiar voice.

The fox rider pulled back his mask. It was Ty.

Giselle gasped. "What? If Ty is the hero then who is the ghost rider?"

"Watch, as I reveal who is really behind the Legend of the Ghost Horse!" exclaimed Callahan.

Everyone held their breath. Callahan pulled off the white hood and goggles. The crowd gasped. It was AMY!!!!

CHAPTER 11

The campers gasped! They couldn't believe it.
Miss Amy was the Ghost Horse rider.

"Why is everyone gasping?" asked Mercedes.
"What's going on? I can't see anything."

Giselle and Mercedes wiggled together,
trying to get out. Evangeline rushed over and
helped them take off the horse costume.

"It was Miss Amy?" realized Mercedes.
"Huh. I did not see that coming."

Giselle let a huge sigh of relief, "I knew Ty
was too cute to be the bad guy."

Ty looked at Giselle and smiled.

"Did I just say that out loud?" asked Giselle,
blushing bright red.

"Can you untie me please?" grumbled Miss
Amy.

Ty helped Amy escape the rope wrapped
around her. Then, she found herself trapped by

Callahan's microphone.

"Night owls, I said it all along, this Ghost Horse was a fake!" lied Callahan to the camera. "This is not the first time I have uncovered someone pretending to be a ghost on my show."

Ty got excited. "Like in episode 54, 'The Savage Rabbit'. And those kids almost got away with it!"

"Almost," said Callahan. "Now everyone, stand back, and get ready to be impressed as I show you how she did it."

The crowd stood quietly, waiting to be entertained by another one of Callahan's stories.

"Most people try to fake a ghost with only spooky sounds at night. Miss Amy, however, took things to the next level to pull off her scam. She created the night chill in the air by the use of a smoke machine and this remote!"

Callahan reached into Amy's shirt pocket and pulled out the remote. The crowd was amazed.

Mercedes whispered to her sisters, "Actually, I discovered that."

Giselle shushed her, "Don't say anything. Remember, no one is supposed to know that we're the Sister Detectives."

Callahan sniffed the Ghost Horse's saddle. "Just as I thought. Glow in the dark paint! The smoke, her white costume, and these glow sticks made us all think we were seeing the real Ghost Horse."

The campers looked at the glow sticks wrapped around the horse saddle. They clapped for Callahan. He had solved the mystery.

Evangeline whispered while she clapped, "We do all the detective work, and he takes all the credit."

"He's such an attention hog," whined Mercedes.

"Takes one to know one," muttered Giselle.

Callahan continued, "You did all of this to pretend to be a ghost. Your campers were terrified. Every night they were too scared to go outside. Because of you, they constantly worried about ghosts lurking in the shadows."

Miss Amy's face filled with regret. She fought back her tears.

Callahan's voice turned serious. "The question on everyone's mind is . . . why? Why did you do it?"

Chief Black Feather walked up to Miss Amy. "Yes my flower, I would like to know. Why did you dishonor our people? How could you betray your family?"

Tears streamed down Miss Amy's cheeks.

"It was never supposed to be like this," cried Miss Amy. "I figured I could fake being the Ghost Horse for a day or two. Callahan would be here and gone before any campers even saw what I was up to. But then, they kept missing the Ghost Horse on video, so I had to keep trying. I never wanted to scare anyone."

Miss Amy stared at the ground. She was too embarrassed to look the chief in the eye.

"The legend of the Warrior Spirit Horse means so much to me," said the chief. "I created this camp to honor the ways of our people."

"I know grandpa, and I love this camp too. But it's dying. We can't live only in the old ways. This place is too run down. We have huge money problems because less campers are coming every year."

Amy's face grew serious.

"If this camp is going to stay open, we need to be like other, newer camps. They have things like computer classes and water slides. The newest thing we have is the broken tire swing at the lake."

Evangeline stepped forward. "Fix it up? What's wrong with the camp? I like it the way it is with all the creepy broken lights and big spooky spiders, and the scary toilets, and the dangerous—"

Miss Amy interrupted, "You just made my point."

Mercedes spoke up, "Not to take Miss Amy's side, but I agree. This place is pretty EW! And you guys don't even have a pool."

"That's what I was going to do with the reward money," explained Amy. "I wanted to get some new stuff and fix things up around here."

"I do not agree," said the chief sternly. "You want to do away with all the activities that focus on our heritage. Computers can't take the place of young ones learning Native American ways."

"No, it's the opposite grandpa," explained Amy. "I don't want to take those things away. I love our heritage and the campers do too."

The crowd of campers nodded in agreement. Some shouted that they loved archery while others went on about how much they loved the forest.

"But a pool would be nice!" added Mercedes.

Everyone agreed with Mercedes.

"Change doesn't have to always be getting rid of the old," said Amy. "We can still keep the old ways and add new things too."

Chief Black Feather looked at Amy, then to the faces of the campers in the crowd.

Amy put her hand on the chief's shoulder. "A wise chief once told me, no one knows where the wind will blow. The earth changes, so we must change with it."

Chief Black Feather sighed. "When did you grow so wise? There is money if we need it. We shall restore these campgrounds and . . . get a pool."

The campers let out a cheer and clapped.

"Plus, you can get a phone," said Amy.

"Don't push it," the chief said with a smile.

The chief gave Amy a hug.

"It feels good to see you mess up for once," said Ty to his big sister.

Amy smiled back. She pulled Ty in for a family hug.

Mercedes grinned at her sisters, "Like I said before, it's always about money sweeties!"

Callahan turned to the camera. "Let this be a lesson. No one can fool the great ghost hunter, Callahan Wilcox. Join us next time, when I travel to the sewers of Paris for a peek at the terrifying, 'Ghostly Gator'. Until then, spooky dreams!"

"And cut," announced Mom. "That's a wrap."

"We make a great team," said Callahan to Mom and Dad. "Want to come with me to Paris? I need a good camera crew."

"You always wanted to go to Paris," Dad said to Mom.

"The sewers of Paris aren't my idea of a fun vacation," answered Mom. "So, no thanks."

"Until we meet again," said Callahan.

He raised his cape covering his face, then walked off, vanishing into the darkness.

"Like I said, that guy is super weird," said Mom.

***

The next day was the best one yet at camp. All the girls from the GEM Sisters' cabin, including Emma, were gathered on Graveyard Hill. They were getting ready to ride horses.

Miss Amy had apologized to Emma and her mom. Not only was Emma staying, but Miss Amy gave her an extra free week of camp to make it up to her.

Mercedes sat at a nearby table, studying her face in the mirror.

"My skin looks so splotchy!" complained

Mercedes.

Chief Black Feather applied medicine to her face with a cotton ball.

"Medicine was created by the Native Americans thousands of years ago," explained the chief. "My people learned which plants can heal a toothache, a spider bite, or even diarrhea."

The chief poured more medicine onto the cotton ball and put it on Mercedes' face. "This medicine helps the itchy skin you got from poison ivy."

Amy watched as the chief helped Mercedes. "Why is the medicine in a bottle you bought from the store?" she asked.

"Like I promised, I'm trying new things. Plus this medicine from the store is pink. And I wanted to make sure that it matched Mercedes' outfit," said the chief with a wink.

Mercedes forced a smile as she peeked in the mirror. It looked like she had polka dots all over her face.

"I'm never going back on the Forbidden Trail," said Mercedes to herself.

"I like your new makeover Mercedes," joked Mom as she walked up.

Mercedes wasn't laughing.

"Your Dad and I want to help film your *Horse Diva's* audition since we're not working anymore," exclaimed Mom.

For a moment, Mercedes was excited. Then she looked at herself in the mirror.

"Ya know what Mom, thanks, but no thanks," said Mercedes.

"But I thought being on that show was your dream," said Mom, confused.

"It is, but today I just want to have fun with my friends," answered Mercedes.

She gave her Mom a hug, then ran off to join the other campers.

"Emma!" shouted Mercedes. "Save a horse for me!"

Over by the group of horses, Ty prepared the saddle for Giselle.

"Hey, I've been wanting to talk to you without your sisters around," said Ty.

"They're always around," replied Giselle with a nervous laugh.

Ty reached out and gently held Giselle's hand.

She looked down at Ty's hand holding hers. Her heart was racing.

"Well, I wanted to say . . ." Ty stopped talking. He cleared his throat. "Sorry, you're just so pretty. You make me really nervous."

He stared into Giselle's eyes. Slowly he leaned in.

Giselle didn't know if she was dreaming. She leaned in and closed her eyes. This was it. They were totally going to kiss.

"Hey there guys!" came Dad's voice as he walked around the horse.

Giselle and Ty quickly pulled away from each other and dropped their hands.

"What's going on?" asked Dad.

"Nothing. You can leave Dad. I think I just heard Mom call you," said Giselle.

Dad gave Giselle a *nice-try* look.

"We were just thinking about going on another sunset trail ride before you all leave tomorrow," said Ty.

"Well that sounds like something I should be there for," answered Dad.

He wrapped his arms around the two of them. "I bet the three of us are going to have a great time! In fact, I'm planning on spending every moment with both of you until we leave."

Giselle groaned. There was no way Dad would leave them alone now. Maybe Ty would wait for her until next year. And maybe, she could come back to camp without her parents!

"Let's go Ty," said Dad. "Come help me pick out a horse."

Miss Amy helped Evangeline onto her saddle.

"Thanks for letting me ride Marshmallow," said Evangeline.

"Actually, his name is Snowflake," explained Miss Amy. "He belongs to my horse trainer from back when Ty and I used to ride in competitions."

Evangeline thought for a second. This was part of the mystery she and her sisters had forgotten to solve. They never asked about where the Ghost Horse had come from.

She decided she didn't really care about the mystery anymore. She was only interested in having fun.

"I'm still gonna call him Marshmallow," said Evangeline.

Evangeline leaned over to pet the horse's mane. "Ah . . . Ah . . . Ah . . . Ah splart!" she sneezed. "Marshmallow you're a genius!"

Giselle and Mercedes rode over on their horses to make sure Evangeline was okay.

"Ah splart! Ah splart!" Evangeline sneezed over and over again.

"Ah splart? Really?" asked Mercedes. "That's

the noise you're going with?"

"I didn't choose the perfect sneeze," answered Evangeline. "It chose me!"

Giselle smiled at her sister. "You are one weird kid."

"Thanks for the compliment," answered Evangeline.

Miss Amy let out a loud whistle. "Okay campers and parents. Now we are going on a special trail ride."

She motioned for everyone to start riding in a line. The campers paid attention to Miss Amy as she spoke.

"As we ride through the forest, I want you to remember that every part of this earth has a purpose," said Miss Amy. "Like us, the earth grows older and wiser. We must never forget the old ways handed down to us by our ancestors. But we must also move forward and be teachers to the new ways of the world."

Chief Black Feather rode on his horse beside Miss Amy. He smiled with pride as she led the campers on the trail ride.

Mom and Dad rode up behind the GEM Sisters.

"I haven't forgotten that you broke my rule about not going to the campfire," said Mom.

"Although that was really clever to sneak in wearing costumes," added Dad.

Dad saw that Mom was giving him a *they're-supposed-to-be-in-trouble* look.

"So when we get home, you're in big trouble," Dad said sternly, trying to impress Mom.

"We'll talk about it later," said Mom. "But right now we need to get our cameras to the front of the line. I told Chief Black Feather we would film more to help out the camp."

The sisters sighed with relief as Mom and Dad rode off. Most likely, they would forget about grounding them when they got home. Their parents were always busy looking for their next project.

"Well a bet's a bet," said Evangeline to Giselle. "You won. The Ghost Horse wasn't real. So did you come up with what I have to wear on my shirt?"

Giselle had worked so hard to solve the mystery that she still hadn't thought of anything. Her mind raced, trying to think of something fast.

A light breeze blew through the trees. A cloud of dust flew off the trail and into Giselle's face. Her eyes closed, and her nose crinkled up.

"Ah splart!" sneezed Giselle.

"Yes! That's a great idea for my shirt!" squealed Evangeline. "I love it!"

"No. I was gonna say—" started Giselle.

"Too late! That's what you said," agreed Mercedes.

"You know what. It's perfect," agreed Giselle.

The Sister Detectives laughed as they rode on the trail.

Giselle, Evangeline, and Mercedes knew solving the mystery of the Haunted Horse Camp was a memory they would share forever.

a GEM Sisters book

Get The Next Mystery!

Support
Sister Detectives!

Leave A Book Review

Tell Your Friends About The Book

Share On Your Social Media

Meet GEM Sisters!
Join the GEM Sisters Club. It's free!
Get updates about a book signing near you!

www.gemsisters.club

About The Authors

MéLisa and Ryun (aka Mama GEM and Papa GEM) have been partners in art and life for over 20 years. Together the authors share a passion for creating funny children and family entertainment for all ages to enjoy. When they are not penning books, they are writing comedy sketches and funny videos with their daughters, GEM Sisters. Check out their popular website www.GEMSisters.club or watch them at youtube.com/gemsisters on YouTube.

Their inspiration for writing books came from encouraging their daughters to love reading as much as they did growing up. After an enthusiastic response from their first book, the authors have now penned multiple series with the wish that young readers everywhere will put down their small screens and open up their imagination. MéLisa and Ryun hope that their books will add a little laughter to your day. Current series include "Spy Pets" and "Sister Detectives".

MORE
Funny Mysteries
By The Authors

For Readers Ages 6-9
Buy Online Wherever Books Are Sold!

Made in the USA
Middletown, DE
13 May 2020